HORSEFLY

ARON BEAUREGARD

BAD DREAM BOOKS

For Daniel J. Volpe

"God knows Himself and every created thing perfectly.
Not a blade of grass or the tiniest insect escapes His eye."

— Mother Angelica

IMPORTANT

Horsefly is an Immersive Entertainment Experience. There are several sections in the book where you will be asked to scan QR codes. You will then be drawn into a cinematic experience that compliments the writing. No AI was used to create this book, the associated artwork, or any of the animations. Please scan the following QR code and watch the short video to ensure you get the best possible reading experience.

If you have any issues scanning the QR codes, please email: AronBeauregardHorror@gmail.com

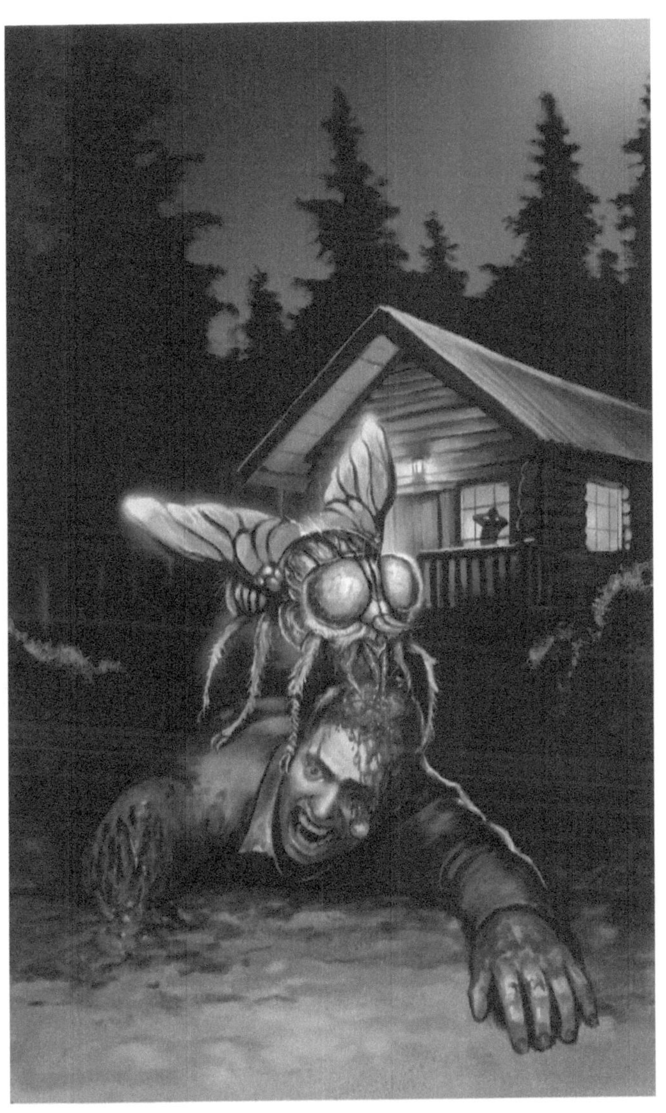

WINGS SPREAD

Man boobs, William Fence thought.

He reached for a napkin and shook his head as he looked out the window of the car. The sun was no joke.

"Is the air conditioner on?" William asked.

"Yes, sir," the driver said.

"Well . . . turn it up, then."

The driver nodded as William reached between the buttons of his shirt with the napkin and tried to absorb the sweat oozing from beneath his fatty pectorals. When he felt the paper grow soggy, he couldn't help but think about the protester outside of one of his laboratories in the city.

Several weeks prior, the sign-wielding environmental maniac had shouted at him, poking fun at his "man boobs." At the time, William had done his best to act like it didn't bother him. But now, he couldn't stop thinking about his moist rack.

When the car entered the facility, he didn't even have to flash his credentials. He was William Fence—his public persona was recognizable to most Americans and even residents of other countries. The appearance he'd cultivated was distinct enough that the guards took one look at his Coke-bottle glasses, poindexter haircut, and, of course, his man boobs, and waved him through.

After the car coasted past several buildings, it finally slowed to a stop. He'd tried his best to sop up the fluid from his leaky pores, but the sweat stains on his shirt wouldn't be missed. He got out of the vehicle, trying not to think about it, and pressed the buzzer on the side of the door impatiently.

"Goddamnit!" Carl Simmons yelled, ripping open the door. "I told you already not to disturb—oh . . ." Fear blossomed in his pupils. "Mr. Fence, I'm terribly sorry. I didn't realize it was—"

"Cut the crap, Carl," William said in his unmistakable tone that made him sound like he was holding his nose when he spoke. "I don't have time for apologies or excuses. Just tell me we're on schedule."

Carl bit his lip a moment, then raised his eyebrow as he figured his wording. "Kind of?"

"What does that mean?" He stepped inside the building, frowning, already annoyed with the semantics.

Carl scratched the side of his face. "Maybe I should just show you."

"There's a lot of money on the line here, and we're running out of time," William said.

Carl led him down the corridor into the lab. As William entered, he wasn't prepared for what confronted them. At the center of the room stood a transparent container the size of a big-screen television.

William gazed through the glass upon the hideous creature.

The horsefly was enormous. The greenish glow around the insect shone even in the light. With a medium-size pig in its clutches, its razor-sharp mouth scissors carved deep into the animal's tender tissue. The gaping slit offered an outpouring of crimson that the fly eagerly lapped from with its bristly tongue. Drool oozed out of the pig's mouth as it went limp and stopped fighting.

William took notice of the brown liquid oozing from the oversized anus of the horsefly and cringed.

"God, what is that awful smell?" he asked.

"That's her waste," Carl said. "The sporadic defecation on her prey while she feeds is a side effect, and unfortunately, the foul scent of her waste has grown along with her frame."

William shuddered. "Why is it so . . . big?"

"Well, that's the problem," Carl said. "Everything else works just the way we wanted it to. Before the horsefly's growth spurt, Disease X transferred to the bitten without issue. The aftereffects on the human subjects, horses, and other livestock included brain fog, fatigue, severe agitation, psychosexual behavior, vomiting, diarrhea, spontaneous aggressive actions, and enough irregular pain spells that any person with half a brain would most certainly be motivated to seek out preventive treatment than be sandbagged with such ailments. I mean, just knowing these symptoms have a possibility of fucking up people's summer nights will move the vaccine."

"What exactly is psychosexual behavior?" William asked.

"It means that their sexual experiences are deeply intertwined with their emotional states."

William scoffed and glared at Carl. "Seriously? We wanted something simple. Something that was more of a nuisance than anything. This was about pushing the shots on the farmers and, primarily, their animals, but these symptoms sound much messier than anything we mapped out."

"That's fair, but I assure you Dr. Cruise has been working on turning their intensity down. She feels confident that we can have everything sorted by the target timeline."

"Good. But just make sure we're *extra* careful. Releasing the disease in such a state might not be the smartest idea."

"I wouldn't worry about that anyway . . ."

"Why?"

"The horsefly hasn't been able to transfer the disease since its surge in size."

"Why's that?"

"Because . . ." Carl said, gulping down his spit, "she's killed everything she's bitten."

An awkward beat of silence ensued before William sighed. "We need to work through this triage quickly."

"But why is there such a strict timeline?"

William pushed his glasses up his greasy nose. "Because every minute, we're losing money. I didn't generate billions just waiting around. I did it lighting fires! We need Disease X introduced, like, yesterday! I might even be willing to say fuck it and roll with the crazy side effects, but we can't release a glowing horsefly the size of a goddamn pit bull into the wild and make it look natural, now, can we?!"

Carl shook his head.

"And why's that?" William asked.

"Because it doesn't look natural," Carl whispered.

"Right! It'd be pretty fucking obvious that someone whipped this thing up in a lab!"

"Of course. I wasn't suggesting that—"

"We picked horseflies so we'd have more control." William pointed at the tank. "This doesn't look like control. Lyme disease got out before we wanted it to and spread like wildfire before we even had the treatments lined up and the patents in place. While it made us some money, it was largely a missed opportunity. And on top of Lyme being leaked, it didn't have enough downside to *really* scare people."

"I haven't forgotten," Carl said. "I'm aware that we bungled it."

William tried to exhale his aggravation, but it was no use. "And that bungle cost *millions*. I was a young man back then. With the wisdom I've accumulated since, I refuse to make the same stupid mistakes. So let me ask you again, then, since you ignored my initial question: Why is the fly so fucking big?!"

"If I was to hypothesize, I'd say it has to do with the steroid treatment I was forced to give it. The initial horseflies were exploding, just ripping apart at the seams, when I infected them with Disease X. I quickly learned that it was due to the extreme inflammation that the virus causes upon initial circulation. But I did something different with this one. Instead of waiting, I juiced her up with a preemptive steroid treatment."

"And?"

"And this time, she absorbed Disease X without incident. Additionally, Dr. Cruise was able to solve the problem—but it was after the fact."

"How so?"

"She edited Disease X—our lab samples and the infection inside the horsefly—and removed the severe inflammation symptom. So, despite her size"—Carl pointed toward the massive creature—"if the disease were to somehow be transferred from her, the extreme swelling wouldn't be an issue."

William stared at him, waiting for more details.

"Another way of saying that is, if we were to foster a new horsefly, she would not require the steroid treatment to survive transmission. While her exponential growth and extreme influx in appetite is concerning, it's not something we'll ever have to worry about again."

The fly continued to eagerly lap up more of the pig's blood. The long, rough licks grated in William's brain like a nail scraping against enamel. As he watched the creature's sawtooth continue to callously shred through the pig's carcass, he shuddered.

"Has she always been this aggressive?" he asked.

"Before I experimented on her, she was housed with several other female and male horseflies. They frolicked a bit, and let's just say that, even back then, she was still the alpha."

"And how extreme was the shift in her consumption?"

"To be blunt, it's like nothing I've ever seen in nature. I can hardly keep up with it. Even when, judging by the sheer volume of the feed, she should no longer be hungry, she still eats."

William bit his fingernail. "Christ . . . well, don't just stand there like a mute imbecile! Tell me how you're fixing it!"

Pointing at the tank, Carl took a few steps closer as the horsefly stopped drinking. He watched carefully as the creature grew sluggish before falling over on its side. The insect lay motionless.

"Well, Dr. Cruise has given her a few experimental injections over the last several days," Carl said. "It's possible that the effects may still be reversable, and we can avoid rebooting the entire run. But it may add a couple of weeks to the study."

"Weeks?!"

"Unfortunately, sir."

"Where the hell is Dr. Cruise, anyway? I'd like to ensure that she's properly motivated."

"She's in the crapper."

"Of course she is." He scoffed. "Fucking women."

William watched as Carl closed in on the horsefly's enclosure and lifted the top off.

"Whoa, whoa, whoa, are you out of your goddamn mind? Didn't we just talk about being *extra* careful?"

Carl picked up an extra-long needle and climbed a stepstool positioned beside the tank. "Relax. That pig was full of enough horse tranquilizer to put out a rhino. She'll be out for at least an hour. I just need to grab a quick sample for analysis."

William nodded, still uneasy. "Make it *extra* quick."

Carl leaned inside the tank, guiding the needle into the horsefly's body. "You know, since you're in town, you should do a little sightseeing. That's the good thing about these clandestine facilities. They're always in the middle of nowhere—suffocated by silence and nature."

"I'm not sure I have time," William said.

"If time's the issue, Mount Archer is only about thirty minutes awa—"

As Carl inserted the needle into the horsefly, it suddenly came to life. The sound of its buzzing wings was deafening.

"Holy shit!" William screamed.

The horsefly knocked Carl backward. He went flying off the stepstool and landed on top of William. The back of his head smacked into William's mouth and busted his lip.

Carl let out a shriek and cried, "No! W-wait—"

The massive insect pounced on the scientist's cranium as soon as it landed. Curling its hairy legs around his torso, it jammed its long, blood-slicked feeding spike into Carl's forehead. The tip of the rod slammed through his head, penetrating his skull and ejecting brains out around the surrounding wound.

As the horsefly's feeding once again commenced, so did its defecation. The Disease X symptoms were on full display as the gelatinous brown sludge drained from the puckering anus of the beast. The rectal reservoir oozed, staining Carl's entire midsection.

William's screams were cut short by the knotty clumps of wet pink that leaked down, accompanied by a surge of hot blood. When the pieces of Carl's cranium found William's open mouth, he immediately choked.

Turning to his side, William coughed several times before spitting the still-quivering wads out of his mouth. The otherworldly scent of the creature's acidic waste stung his nostrils. The smell of dead maggots, urine, and excrement drizzled off Carl's body and saturated William's three-hundred-dollar slacks. He could instantly sense the disgusting warmth of the fecal matter seeping into his skin and irritating his flesh.

Feeling Carl's death tremors as he vibrated atop him like an eager stripper giving a lap dance, William found himself too frightened to scream. While the gushing gore slimed William's upper body, he remained too terrified to move.

In the reflection of the steel table, he saw the side of the horsefly's frame throb as it harvested the scientist's essence. The pulsating, bee-like body continued to inflate as the monstrous creature slurped more blood from Carl's body.

Searching for more succulence, the horsefly dragged its saw-like mouthpart from the crown of Carl's head down to his throat. As the slicing burrowed deeper, William watched as the left and right halves of Carl's face flapped agape on each side of his head like a greeting card being opened.

It took several more seconds for the horsefly to finish its gorge. But once it had its fill, William heard the wings flutter again. The maddening sound was a hundred times more intense than a bee buzzing by his ear. As the glowing, blood-drenched creature levitated, William stared silently into the manic eyes of the unhinged insect. They were like two mini moons covered in ultra-thin mesh.

The horsefly turned to the far end of the room, angling itself toward the door. Staring at the barrier, the creature eagerly buzzed. It quickly descended again and wrapped its glistening legs around Carl's twitching carcass.

William scurried away like a terrified cockroach, hiding behind a lab table. He looked on in fear as, in an absurd feat of strength, the horsefly lifted Carl's mangled body off the ground. Then, like a charging bull, the creature launched full speed ahead. The glowing beast flung the corpse into the door, and a sickening crunch of bone echoed. Carl's flayed face left a giant wet ruby kiss on the door as his body slid down and thudded to the ground.

A tremor of terror exploded inside William.

God . . . help me . . .

The thought was a difficult one for William to allow. He wasn't the type of man to beg God for help—he was the type of man who wanted to play God. But as the horsefly picked Carl's corpse off the ground again, William knew his billions of dollars would do him little good in the face of such extreme danger. He nervously brushed the blood and brain matter off his cheek and tried to wipe the bug shit off his itchy legs.

In a flash, the scientist's body had been launched into the door again, this time, the velocity of the impact causing the door to break open. Carl's pulverized body lay in the doorway, propping it open. After the alarms sounded throughout the building, William mustered the strength to approach the door. He peered around the corner and down the hallway, realizing there was no longer a reason to hide.

The horsefly was gone.

CHOSEN

As the massive horsefly buzzed through the trees, the insatiable hunger inside propelled her onward. She slowed as she came upon the lake and the trees that arched over the water.

Brrrrt-zzuuuumm-bzzzz! she thought.

It was perfect! The space was exactly what she'd pictured in her head. She'd found the environment that would help her do what came naturally. The horsefly was flabbergasted that she'd been able to find an ideal space with such ease. It was almost as if it was meant to be.

Something else that was meant to be was her escape. Being out of captivity didn't feel like an accident; it felt more like divine intervention. The humans had held her in that box against her will for a long time, and while she still wasn't sure why they'd kept her there, something was clearly different. It wasn't just her size; there was also a feeling inside her—something that she didn't know how to express.

When the horsefly fed on animals in the wild, as she'd done several times already, she didn't feel groggy and go to sleep right after her bloodmeals anymore. In fact, if anything, she had *more* energy. But with that energy came other things . . . things that she wasn't sure how to feel about.

The feeling of overwhelming rage was attached to a perverted lust for violence. She didn't understand why she was so mad, but that didn't seem to matter. The uncontrollable urge to act on the feelings possessed her.

Still, she couldn't help but be curious about these feelings that she grappled with. As the horsefly took off into the sky and whizzed through the trees, she tried to figure out what was making her tick in such a way. It wasn't so much about survival or nourishment anymore. It was about tearing her prey apart—mutilating them in a way that made living past their interaction impossible.

Buuuurrrrrt-hhhzzzz-mmmzzz?

Why was she so angry? Why was she so dedicated to destruction? The urge was always egging her on, and the idea was always on her mind.

The horsefly landed on a tree branch that wasn't too far from a sign that read CAMP HAWK. Off in the distance, a tiny dog growled and barked. It was as if the animal could sense her dark presence. It was impeccable timing for the horsefly.

Because she was *always* hungry.

SOMETIME
LATER

A FEW MILES OUT

LeeAnn Sanders looked out the window as the car passed a sign almost hidden by several tree branches.

"Look at that, Mount Archer's only another twenty-five miles away," Zach said.

She could tell by her boyfriend's tone that he was a little anxious too.

"So . . . I guess we're really doing this, then," LeeAnn said.

Sensing her nervousness, Zach was quick to offer an out. "We're not there yet. It's not too late for us to turn around."

LeeAnn thought back to the night when she'd come out of her shell. It was the week after her twenty-ninth birthday, when she'd sat down in the living room with a deathly serious expression.

"Jeez, what's wrong?" Zach had asked, wide-eyed. "Did someone die or something?"

He was partly right. She wasn't mourning a person but the death of her youth. The death of the curiosity and experimentation that LeeAnn knew she'd never experience again. Unless she had the difficult discussion with Zach.

Just the thought of their talk that night made her cringe. She'd expected him to be furious. They'd been together since seventh grade. All they'd ever known was each other.

For LeeAnn to suggest something so radical, something that would most certainly rock the entire foundation of their relationship and even potentially end it, would've upset most people.

But Zach was different. He listened to her. He remained calm. And shockingly, he'd even agreed with her.

Could they really both go their entire lives without knowing another person's touch outside of each other? They both agreed that maybe it was better to face the question head-on. Get all the demons out of their systems in the light, together, instead of betraying each other and tiptoeing around in a world laced with lies and deception.

Still, despite their agreement on the issue, for LeeAnn, there was a certain weirdness in the air. The idea that there was zero pushback from Zach almost made her second-guess the entire thing. The discomfort she thought would be owned by Zach, she now shared with him. But with that discomfort also came excitement.

The swingers bar, Lucky's, where they'd initially tried to mingle, was a little strange at first. They had no idea what they were doing, but after just a short time, LeeAnn and Zach were approached by a trio of open-minded people.

Ruben, Whitney, and Gen were all very cool, and over a few drinks, they'd gotten to know them some. The interaction was natural and fun. LeeAnn and Zach came away feeling like they'd been hanging out with a group of good-looking friends rather than some people they needed to try and woo.

Another thing they both liked was that they weren't pushy. Ruben, Whitney, and Gen weren't looking at them like meat for the taking just because they were at a swingers bar. Everything was always calm and casual, the conversations more about interests and current events than solely rooted in sex and flirtation.

This approach was appreciated by both LeeAnn and Zach. Since neither of them had ever tried anything so unconventional, they were very nervous. After their meetups, they'd always confide in each other, wondering if what they were doing was right or if they even still wanted to continue forward with it.

The charming personalities and relaxed atmosphere the trio fostered made it difficult for them not to want to keep meeting up. Slowly, LeeAnn and Zach moved ahead, attending over a half-dozen hangouts.

Until the night Ruben made them an offer.

It wasn't anything crazy. He just asked them if they might be interested in a cabin retreat with a few other like-minded friends. People who were all cool and relaxed, just like them, as well as open to any idea, should one happen to arise. Ruben was a sexy, charming guy. LeeAnn would've been lying to herself if she said she hadn't thought about him a few times alone in the shower.

"Did you hear me?" Zach asked.

LeeAnn broke away from her thoughts, returning to their drive to the secluded cabin retreat. But her heart remained racing from just thinking about getting the opportunity to see Ruben again.

"Um . . ." she said. "Sorry. It's just all kind of intense, don't you think? I'm excited, but . . . just a little nervous, I guess."

"I'm nervous too," Zach said. "But like we agreed from the beginning, just because we show up doesn't mean we have to stay there. If it gets too weird, or if we're not feeling the vibe, we can always just leave. Whitney said that everyone going is super cool, though. It's all people we've met at Lucky's one time or another, so it shouldn't be weird."

LeeAnn raised her eyebrow. "When did you talk to Whitney?"

"This morning. She called the house while you were in the shower."

An awkward silence lasted a beat before Zach pivoted the conversation. His eyes darted to the speeding ticket stuffed into the console.

"Can't believe they clocked us out here," Zach grumbled. "We're in the middle of nowhere."

LeeAnn shook her head. "I know. Three hundred fucking dollars is insane."

"You think your uncle can take care of it?"

"I doubt it."

"Why not?"

"We're in a different state, babe. Just because he's a cop doesn't mean he knows every cop in the country."

"Still, it's worth a try."

LeeAnn stayed quiet. There was a seed of jealousy growing in her belly. She was still thinking about Whitney calling. She tried to push past it. After all, the entire thing was her own idea. She knew that her jealousy was misplaced. But as Zach hit his turn signal for the exit, something else suddenly bothered her.

"Hmm . . ." she mumbled.

"What is it?" Zach asked.

"I'm . . . I'm just still not sure, I guess. I mean, how well do we actually know these people?"

As Zach took the exit, he laughed.

LeeAnn smiled. Something about him chuckling comforted her. "What's so funny?"

"You think I wouldn't protect you?" He shook his head. "I feel like sometimes you forget that I box. In fact, I've had more boxing matches than you've had birthdays." Holding up his fist, he flexed his bicep and bobbed his head.

"Yeah, but how many'd you win?"

Zach sucked his teeth and brushed off the comment. "No one's record is perfect. But if anyone fucks around with us, they'll wish they didn't."

Another laugh escaped LeeAnn as she recalled the pictures of him in his late teens looking like Rocky Balboa. While, as of late, Zach only hit the heavy bag from time to time, his even-keeled nature made her forget how badass he could be if he needed to.

Thinking about Zach's physical prowess brought LeeAnn the reassurance she needed. She'd only seen him fight once, when they were younger. It was at a house party that had gotten out of hand. A couple of guys started getting rowdy, but Zach had been quick to put them both on the floor.

Recalling the pair of drunk idiots that he'd put to sleep in seconds made her wonder if he secretly looked forward to the occasional confrontation. Regardless, that memory alone was enough to put her at ease.

"Okay, Rocky," LeeAnn said. "Now I definitely feel better." She reached into the backseat. "But do you know when I'll really feel better?"

He paused, seeming almost afraid to ask. "When?"

"When my butt is parked in this baby!"

She held up the portable hammock. The bag that contained the net wasn't big, but the picture on the front showed a couple lounging together in total comfort with huge smiles on their faces.

"Whoa, nice grab," Zach said.

LeeAnn smiled. "So, are you gonna *hang* with me?"

"As long as it's just you and me in there . . . I don't see why not."

She wondered if Zach thought she wanted to do sexual things with a group. The way he'd answered her made her feel that way. LeeAnn hoped he didn't think she was trying to push for some kind of orgy.

The trickiest part about their situation was that neither of them felt comfortable discussing it deeply. The details were foggy. Since there hadn't been a lot of clarity to their early talks, it had left room for speculation. But it was such a new and uncomfortable topic that LeeAnn wasn't sure how to go about explaining exactly what she wanted.

"Yeah," she said with a nod. "The hammock is just you and me."

But the bed . . . she thought, picturing Ruben's handsome face. *The bed's another story.*

THE RETREAT

Sydney Holms stared at the beautiful slice of farmland as several horses roamed freely inside the wooden fence. The white and cream-colored one stuck out. While she loved animals, at the same time, they brought her back to the reason she'd run away.

"Hey, Milk!" a male voice yelled.

The combination of her ultra-pale skin and growing up working on farms earned her the nickname. Turning toward the cabin, she saw Austin and Nina walking around the front of the property.

Austin still had a full head of dark hair, but his wrinkles were starting to show. It was obvious that he was the oldest person in their group, most likely in his mid-forties, but that didn't matter much. He was still young at heart and fit in well with everyone. Nina probably assisted him with that to some extent. Just having a sexy girlfriend at his side who was at least ten years his junior helped Austin blend in. While Milk hadn't known them for long, she felt they were good people. They might've been a little emotionally mixed-up, but they didn't rub her the wrong way.

We're all a little mixed-up, I guess, Milk thought. *That's the whole reason we're here.*

As Austin and Nina came closer, Milk smiled at them. "What's up?"

"Ruben asked us to grab some firewood and kindling for later tonight," Austin said. "Do you feel like helping?"

"Of course."

"Awesome," Austin said. "Can you believe this place?"

"It sure is something special," Milk said.

"You can say that again," Nina said. "All he does is complain about school, but since we got out here, not a peep."

Milk furrowed her brow. While she knew it was never too late to learn, she was surprised that Austin, a man on the backside of forty, would still be taking classes.

"What are you studying?" Milk asked.

"Oh, ha, I'm not *in* school," Austin corrected. "I just oversee one. I'm the principal of a middle school. If it was merely my education at stake, I wouldn't be anywhere near as stressed as I am."

"I'm sure the stress will be worth it," Milk said. "You're shaping lives. That's honorable."

"You're very kind," Austin said, looking toward the forest. "Well, I'm gonna get started. Why don't you tell *her* that." He pointed at Nina before scurrying to the outskirts of the property.

Nina laughed and turned back to Milk. "What a fool. He thinks he deserves a medal or something for having a job. I teach there too, but you don't hear me asking for a pat on the back every five minutes."

"You don't strike me as a teacher," Milk said. "So you know what that means, right?"

"What?"

"You're probably the coolest one."

"You're a doll," Nina said, approaching the fence beside her and watching the horses in the distance.

"Look at that," Milk said, pointing.

They could see the massive mountain off in the distance. A ways beyond the highland, elevated well into the sky, stood a watchtower. The tall wooden structure looked a bit weathered.

Nina spotted the structure. "That's something else. Must be cool to work up there."

"As much as I love nature, I don't think I could." Milk shyly bit her fingernail.

"Why's that?"

She saw the answer in her mind: the long fall to the ground from the upper level of the barn . . . the heavy rain pouring down as his rough hands dangled her petite body over the edge, threatening to let her fall . . . her rotund belly poking out as she looked down and heard his voice . . .

I'll send you both to Hell, bitch, he'd promised.

"Milk?" Nina persisted.

She came back from the dark memory. "Um . . . I guess heights just aren't my thing."

Nina brandished a sly smirk and leaned in a little closer. "Well, you never know. Sometimes people change." She arched her back slightly, pushing her tan breasts closer to Milk. "You may be a little scared or intimidated, but you won't know if you can handle it—or maybe even like it—until you've tried it."

Feeling her face getting hot, Milk knew the blush was probably coming on strong. Because of her complexion, it was always extra visible.

"Good point," she said, giggling.

She hoped the laugh would help break up the awkwardness. Part of her was excited about Nina's frisky ways, but another part felt uncomfortable. She found herself searching for a distraction and was grateful when an opportunity presented itself.

"Don't move," Milk whispered.

"W-what's going on?" The dread in Nina's voice was thick. "You're freakin' me out."

"Just stay still."

With the swiftness of a gunslinger, Milk's hand vaulted up to Nina's shoulder and cupped around it. Nina jumped back as Milk gently maneuvered her fingers.

"What the hell is that?!" Nina asked.

"It's a horsefly." Milk held the plump pest between her fingers and grabbed hold of its wings. "These are nasty suckers. Trust me, you don't want to deal with a bite from one of these things all weekend."

As Nina took in the oversized eyes and ferocious mouth of the insect, she shuddered.

Milk pinched the horsefly's wings between her fingers and yanked, tossing the de-winged pest onto the ground.

"Why'd you do that?" Nina asked.

"I don't like killing anything . . . At least this way, she's still alive but not harassing us"—Milk looked up and nodded at the horses—"or them the entire time."

Nina laughed. "So, you don't like killing things . . . but you're okay with sentencing them to a slow and torturous life of agony?"

Shrugging, Milk returned the smile. "Do you have a better solution?"

"I guess not," Nina conceded. "Well, I guess we should probably start looking for that wood. I'll see you around. Happy hunting."

Milk nodded. "Yeah, see you around."

As Nina ran off in the direction of Austin, Milk turned back to the farm. She took in the ranch, admiring the cozy house, oversize barn, and small windmill in the distance.

Stop thinking about the past. Focus on what's in front of you, she thought.

She pivoted her gaze from the property, watching the horses calmly use their tails to swat away other flies from their backsides.

It must suck to not have hands.

Milk walked around the outskirts of the fence and noticed a fair amount of dry timber where the woods began. As she bent to pick up some branches, she noticed a metallic spout had been hammered into the tree in front of her.

"Weird," she mumbled to herself.

"It's a tree tap," a gruff voice said, suddenly manifesting behind her.

Startled, Milk turned to see an older man in a cowboy hat with a stiff look on his face.

"Oh, neat," she said. "What's it do?"

"In the late winter months, I used it to drain the maple sap. I haven't used it in a few seasons, though. I suppose I've already got enough maple syrup in my basement to last me through this life and the next."

She grinned. "Well, there's nothing wrong with being prepared."

"When you're as far from civilization as I am, you gotta stockpile everything."

She nodded but didn't know what else to say.

"I apologize for startling you," the man continued. "I promise I'm not coming over here to harass you."

"I didn't think that at all," she replied.

"Truth is, I don't mean to come off any kind of way, but . . . the property line ends back there." He pointed several yards in the other direction.

"Oh, gosh," she said. "I'm so sorry—I didn't mean to invade your property."

"It's all right. You don't seem like a lot of the other folks who come and stay at that cabin and raise hell." The man approached her and offered his hand. "Name's Wayne."

She shook his hand. "Nice to meet you. I'm Milk. I'm glad I didn't come off disrespectful. I certainly didn't mean to."

"Your name's . . . Milk?"

"Yeah. Well, my nickname."

Wayne walked back past the fence, guiding her to the property line.

"You know, when I bought this little ranch, I thought it was gonna be a nice, quiet retirement for me. I never imagined having new neighbors every week." He sighed and shook his head. "That slimeball realtor never told me I was moving next to a goddamn rental."

Milk grimaced, not knowing how to respond. Trying to politely change the subject was the only thing she could seem to think of.

"That sounds tricky . . . I used to be a farmhand too. It's how I grew up and what I did for a long time after. I know what it can be like having unwanted people spoiling your serenity. But other than the out-of-towners, do you like living this way?"

Wayne nodded. "It's just me and the horses." He leaned over the fence. "But that's the way I like it. I've shifted to a minimalist lifestyle. No car, no TV, no phone, just me and Mother Nature." He licked his lips, staring at the muscular white horse in the center of the field. "Without any distractions, I've got extra time to spoil my Sweet Cream."

Milk nodded at the horse. "Is that her name?"

"His."

"Nice. Well, I guess that's kind of the point of being out here. There's a TV and VCR in our cabin, but I don't plan on using them. I'm glad there's no phone either, although I doubt anyone would be calling me. But what about if there's an emergency? Is it just our cabin and your ranch out here?"

He pointed at the watchtower in the distance. "Aside from them. I guess if something crazy happened to me, the forest rangers would be my closest link to society."

"That's cool. Are you guys, like, friends?"

Wayne let out a short chuckle. "Those guys are a couple of bozos."

She looked at him and nodded, feeling like her social battery had already been drained. Milk didn't enjoy talking to men she didn't know, but considering she'd accidently encroached on Wayne's land, she'd gone out of her way to be polite. He seemed nice enough, and ruining the weekend was the last thing she wanted to come out of the interaction.

"Okay, well, maybe I'll see you around," she said, turning her attention to the ground and looking for more sticks.

Wayne tipped his cowboy hat. "If all goes well, you won't have to."

EYE IN THE SKY

Her cleavage was right between the crosshairs.

Jared Myers gawked at the woman's melons. As she bent over to pick up wood, he'd picked up some wood of his own. The erection in his pants continued to rise.

"Fucking tits are massive," he said, licking his lips.

An older-looking man entered the scope. He stood in front of the busty woman, and they exchanged words.

"Ugh, this faggot is blocking my view!"

"Dude," another voice said, "how many times do I gotta tell you, you can't just point a gun at a chick because you wanna check out her rack. Every day, it becomes more clear why the State Troopers passed on you."

Jared looked away from the scope, glaring at his coworker, Toby Reynolds. The handkerchief covering his receding hairline was moist with sweat, and his sunglasses were dirty.

"Staties are a bunch of pussies and queers," Jared snarled. "They're just afraid of having a *true* alpha on their squad."

"Right . . . Just keep telling yourself that."

"At least I have aspirations. What's your goal, smartass?"

Toby removed a joint from the top pocket of his ranger uniform and lit it. He took a puff so big that it made him immediately cough out some of the smoke.

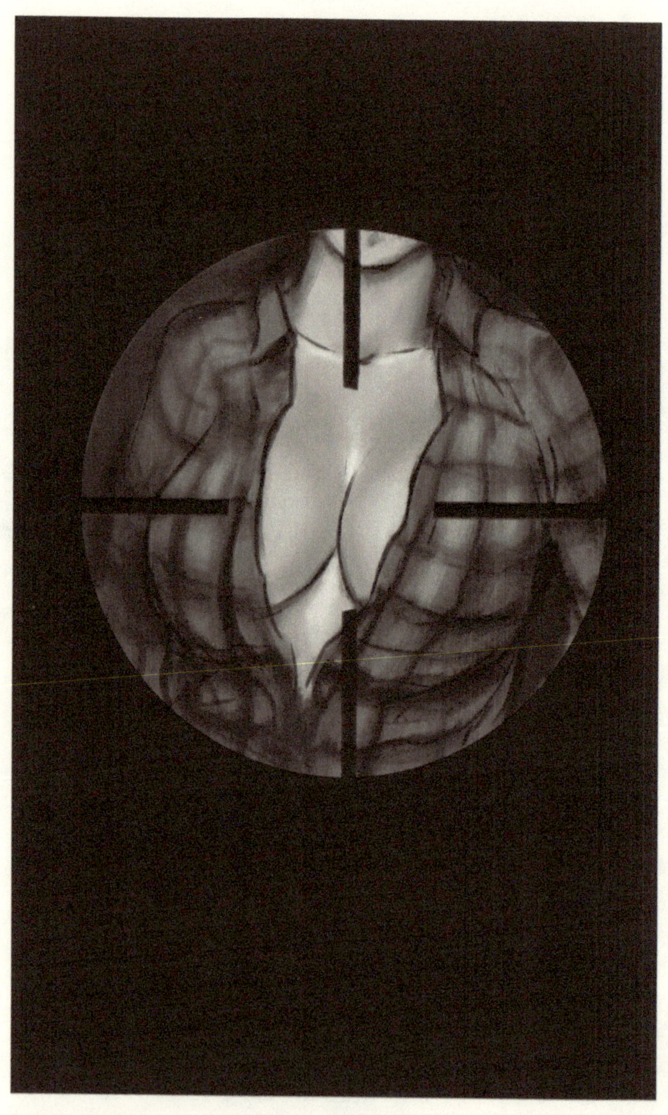

"You're looking at it, brother," he finally managed.

Jared scoffed. "Look at you."

"What?"

"Listen, you know I love you, man. But you're sitting around here most of the time with the mental capacity of a retarded child. You're just looking at stuff . . . and hungry. It's supposed to be puff, puff, pass, but with you, it's puff, puff, until you pass out."

"Dude, that's because you never wanna smoke with me." Toby French inhaled his next hit. "If you'd just fucking partake once in a while, maybe I wouldn't have to go so hard, you know what I'm saying?"

"You just don't get it." Jared shook his head like a disappointed father.

Toby coughed out another cloud of smoke. "Hey, man, I'm just here chilling. I ain't hurting anybody. I don't know why you always gotta be judging me."

"You know what your fucking problem is?"

"I can't wait to hear this."

"Your problem is that you're always too zooted to think about the big picture."

"Please, tell me about the 'big picture.' I love photography."

"You should be happy—jumping for fucking joy—that I'm here holding shit down with my head on straight. If something went sideways out here, you're too much of a sissy to lay down the law."

"So I don't like guns," Toby said. "Big deal."

"It's more than just that. You're afraid of confrontation. But that's what you signed up for."

"We're fucking forest rangers, dude."

Jared stomped his foot. "You took an oath!"

"C'mon, it's not like anything ever happens out here anyway." Toby took in another massive hit of the joint. "This job is tit, and that's why I'm the perfect guy for it."

"Just because nothing's happened yet doesn't mean you shouldn't always be prepared."

"And outside of scoping melons, how are you preparing for this fictional incident?"

"You act like I do it just for the boners, but there's more to it than that. When I've got a nice pair of melons in my crosshairs, I'm practicing my aim, keeping steady, and regulating my breathing. You wouldn't know what it takes to shoot, though. You're too much of a liberal coward—bleeding heart and all."

"Man, don't stick me with that label. I can't be defined by a label. I ain't shit."

"*That* I can actually agree with."

Toby pointed to his head. "This mind isn't captured by any ideology. This mind is *free*. I'm just a dude who wants to smoke and be left alone."

Jared raised the rifle again and started to scan the area around the cabin. "And that's the difference between us. You want simple satisfaction." He keyed in on the girl's cleavage again. "And I want action."

THE TRINITY

"Do you think they'll be down?" Ruben Alto asked.

He watched Whitney and Gen continue to put food away in the fridge and pantry of the cabin. They were the two he trusted the most—his left and right hand. Everything had started with the three of them, but now they'd branched out. To keep the lifestyle they craved afloat, they had no choice but to.

"Nina will," Gen said.

Ruben stroked his chin. "How did she respond when the two of you linked up?"

"She gets loose fast."

"Good." Ruben turned to Whitney. "And what about Austin?"

"I can't say for sure." Whitney grabbed a beer from the fridge, opened it, and took a sip. "When he drove me home, I tried to suck his dick, but he didn't want it."

"Maybe if you hit the gym once in a while, you might get some interest," Gen said, looking at her painted nails.

Whitney glared at her. "Bitch, you wish you was thick like this with those chicken legs."

"Girls," Ruben said.

They both went quiet.

He looked at Whitney. "You brought the juice, right?"

She nodded, but the wrinkles in her forehead concerned Ruben. He could see she still wasn't totally on board.

"I don't have a good feeling about this," Whitney finally said. "Maybe we should—"

"I didn't ask you to feel," Ruben said. "I didn't ask you to think, or to ask questions, or make suggestions. Leave all the schematics to me. Get me a beer."

Gen quickly snatched a can out of the fridge before Whitney could and brought it to him.

"Have a seat." Ruben said. "Both of you."

The girls sat on the loveseat adjacent from him, awaiting his words.

"Have I failed either of you before?" Ruben asked.

They both shook their heads.

"Things have been pretty fucking good since you joined up with me, right?" he asked.

They both nodded.

He looked at Gen. "You miss picking up dirty singles after your song's up?"

"No, I wasn't questioning y—"

"That was a 'yes' or 'no,' bitch." Ruben's glare shifted to Whitney. "You miss fucking all them unvetted strangers to make rent?"

"No," Whitney replied.

"Then I suggest the two of you appreciate what I rescued you from and trust the process that got you this far. This life ain't free. Sacrifices have to be made. But what I ask of you isn't unreasonable. Hell, you're both freaks. I know you enjoy that shit anyhow." He zeroed in on Whitney. "Now, back to Austin. He's kinda fuckin' old. You think maybe he's just a stiff?"

She shook her head. "That's not the vibe I got."

"Well? Talk to me."

"What it reminded me of was this one guy I used to work with back in the day. He said he wanted to be friends, but whenever we chilled, he didn't want it. Took me a little while to realize it."

"Realize what?" Ruben said.

Whitney took a sip of her beer and burped. "That he was gay."

"Oh . . . shit," Ruben said, computing the revelation in his head. He grinned. "Even better."

Whitney and Gen both seemed confused by his response, but neither questioned it.

"Nina and Austin won't be a problem," Ruben said, taking another drink. "They've been around long enough to follow our lead. But what about Milk? She's almost as new as Zach and LeeAnn. Do you think inviting her was a mistake?"

Whitney kept quiet.

"I think she's perfect," Gen said. "You can tell she's been through something. She's running. She's—"

"Afraid?" Ruben interrupted.

"I think so," Gen said.

Ruben took another gulp of his beer. "Fear is good. It keeps people grounded. It softens them into putty and makes them moldable."

He winked at Gen and glared at Whitney. "I already knew Milk was perfect. I intimately understand her history. I have that girl in the palm of my hand. But I wanted to see who would speak up." He turned back to Gen. "It's good to know you have an eye for the truth."

From the corner of his eye, Ruben noticed a car pulling up the driveway. He shifted his focus to the window, then back to the girls.

"That's gotta be them," he said. "Now remember, don't be talking like hoodrats in front of the new blood. Just like when we see them at the bar. Class it up, understood?"

They both nodded.

Ruben stood from the couch and took another swig of his beer. "Aight, then. It's showtime."

SETTLING IN

"Now that we're finally here, I'm kind of excited," Zach said, parking the car behind a gray sedan and red SUV.

"Yeah, me too," Lee Ann said. "But let's just . . . go slow, especially on this first night. Okay?"

"Of course." He kissed her as he reached for the backpack behind them.

Zach watched as LeeAnn got out of the car.

Just play it cool, he thought. *It'll be all right.*

He took a deep breath and exited the car.

"Hey, what's up, you guys?" Nina said, stepping out of the forest, arms filled with wood up to her cleavage.

"Hey, good to see you again," LeeAnn said, slinging her backpack over her shoulder.

Zach removed a small suitcase from the back of the car. "This place looks killer."

"Wait until you see inside," Austin said, stepping from the tree line. "Nina, let's stack this wood around back." He looked at Zach. "But you guys should head in and check it out."

"Sounds good," Zach said.

"Hi," Milk said, smiling in passing as she followed Nina and Austin around the side of the cabin. "Great to see you guys again."

"You too," LeeAnn said.

Once the three of them had disappeared around the side of the cabin, Zach and LeeAnn looked at each other.

"I guess we should go inside," Zach said.

"Yeah," LeeAnn said. "Here goes nothing."

They both approached the door but didn't get a chance to knock before a familiar face pulled it open.

"Hey there," Ruben said with a big grin. "Come on in! I'm so glad you both could make it."

As Zach followed behind LeeAnn, he could see Whitney and Gen hanging out on the couch. Whitney's low-cut top really showed off her breasts—even more than Nina's. Zach found himself sneaking a peek at them, but he was careful not to let LeeAnn see him.

Why should it even matter? he thought. *Isn't that the point of this? Damn, she looks good . . .*

His relationship with LeeAnn had kept him occupied since high school. He'd always imagined that she would be his first and last, but the latter was now in jeopardy. It worried him just as much as it excited him. Zach had always found Black women incredibly attractive but never had the chance to explore them sexually. The fact that Whitney had already called him to chat would seem to indicate that she was interested. As she stared back at him, biting her bottom lip seductively, he felt even more confident.

When Ruben hugged LeeAnn, he did so respectfully. "Good to see you, Lee."

"Good to see you too," LeeAnn replied.

Zach didn't like him giving her a nickname. It felt like it gave them some kind of connection that circumvented him. LeeAnn was *his* girl—if anyone was going to give her a pet name, it should've been him. But at the same time, he didn't want to stir up shit over nothing.

When Zach gripped Ruben's hand, he squeezed it tight. The gesture was a display of dominance. A reminder that he wouldn't be pushed around. Not that Ruben had ever done that, or even wanted to.

"So, Zach," Ruben said, smiling and gesturing behind him. "What do you think?"

Zach wasn't sure if he was asking about the cabin or talking about his girls. Either way, it all looked good. The cabin looked huge and spacious. And Whitney and Gen looked sexy and horny. They both waved welcomingly at Zach and LeeAnn, and they returned the greeting.

"This is incredible," Zach said. "It looks more like a mansion than a cabin. Are you sure you don't want us to kick in on this?"

"Seriously," LeeAnn added. "We feel bad."

"Absolutely not," Ruben said. "You're our guests! We're just happy to have you with us."

"Are you sure, man?" Zach persisted.

"Positive." Ruben grinned. "But maybe you can help us out with the next one."

"I'm sure we can do that," LeeAnn said.

"Great. Well, your room is upstairs—the last door on the left." Ruben pointed at the staircase. "It has a nice little balcony that looks out into the woods. Why don't you guys go get settled in? Then, once you're done, maybe we can all have lunch together."

"That sounds perfect," LeeAnn said.

"Wait—before you go, let me get a shot of everyone," Gen said, moving behind the couch. She lifted a VHS camcorder off the table. The red light on its side activated. "So, we already took a little video of the place and each of our other guests as they arrived. Here's our last two, Zach and LeeAnn. Are you guys ready to have some fun this weekend?"

"You know it," LeeAnn said, smiling while Zach fist-pumped beside her.

"What a gorgeous couple," Gen said. "I could just shoot the two of you all day—and *all* night . . ."

"All right, Gen," Ruben said. "Enough fun with the camera for now."

"Sorry," Gen said with a chuckle.

"No need to apologize," Ruben said. "But they had a long drive, so we should let them get settled."

"Right on." Zach headed for the stairs, trying to play it cool, but Gen had turned him on. "We'll see you guys in a few."

They ascended the stairs and made their way into their bedroom. Once inside, Zach closed the door behind them and they set their bags down.

"Oh my God, this is amazing!" LeeAnn said, looking through the sliding doors at the wooden balcony. "Look at that view! And we've got our own bathroom!"

"Oh, fuck yeah," Zach said.

LeeAnn moved in, and they kissed passionately, carrying on a bit longer before she pulled away and smiled at him.

"That was nice," Zach said.

"You deserve all the nice things," she said.

"Really? Why's that?"

LeeAnn looked into his eyes adoringly. "Because you didn't judge me for having this idea. You supported me. It just makes me know that being with you is right."

As much as the idea of hooking up with other people excited Zach, it still terrified him. Just because he'd supported LeeAnn's suggestion didn't mean he didn't have reservations about it.

"You got that right." He kissed her again. "Now if you'll excuse me for a second, I've got some overdue business to attend to. This thing's been brewing since we got off the exit . . ."

"Ugh, TMI," LeeAnn said, starting to unpack her bag.

Zach grabbed his backpack, closed the bathroom door, and turned on the light and air vent. Staring into the mirror, part of him was disgusted with his reflection. He might've been a tough guy when it came to fights and bravado, but when it came to LeeAnn, he was as soft as a melted marshmallow.

You're really gonna let them fuck your girl? he thought. *You're not even gonna fight for it?!*

Zach knew he wasn't cut out for arguments. If there was one thing he'd learned about women—and LeeAnn in particular—it was that silence is a better alternative than screaming.

Deep inside, he'd never agreed with the idea that they needed to explore other sexual partners. When LeeAnn had first presented the idea, it had caught him off guard. It felt not only emasculating but embarrassing. The person he'd been with for nearly his entire life had grown so bored of him that she was willing to risk potentially destroying their relationship for a cheap thrill.

You're that boring, bro?

Zach had only agreed to it because he'd thought that it might dissuade LeeAnn. In a way, it was also kind of like respectfully saying, "Oh, so you think *I'm* a bad lay? Well, right back at you. I've been thinking the same about *you*." But she didn't back down.

And playing it cool had brought them out in the middle of nowhere with a glorified group of strangers.

Zach reached into his backpack and pulled out a small, dark blue box. He opened it and looked at the modest diamond that he'd spent years saving for. But before he'd gotten to pop the question, LeeAnn had popped her own.

Maybe she just needs to get it out of her system.

He looked back into the mirror.

Maybe I do too. Once she's been with someone else, we can go back to normal.

Zach exhaled, closed the ring box, and quickly slipped it back into the bag.

Maybe then it'll finally be time to ask my question.

BONFIRE

LeeAnn sat on the blanket, nestled in Zach's arms. As Austin stumbled forward, shooting a stream of lighter fluid into the fire, they all cheered and watched as the flames extended, licking higher and higher.

"Better hope this place has a fire extinguisher," Zach said.

"Right on top of the fridge," Ruben said with a laugh. "But let's try to avoid using it if we can."

"Seriously," Nina said. "Austin, be careful."

Austin's grin remained steady. "What? I'm just having a little fun is all."

"Okay," Ruben said. "It's tradition that when we have one of these little get-togethers, we all do one shot together."

"Yes! Finally," Gen said, finishing off her beer and tossing the can.

Austin, who was already a little bit tipsy, shook his head. "I don't know . . . I don't really do shots."

"Don't be a pussy," Nina said, poking him teasingly.

As LeeAnn watched the two of them, it was clear that they didn't seem to know how to handle their liquor. She looked at the bottle of lighter fluid in Austin's hand and wondered if he should be playing with such things while he was so clearly inebriated.

"It's just one," Ruben said. "You don't have to do any more for the rest of the weekend. We do it more as a symbol of our unity than anything else."

Nina elbowed him.

"Okay . . . but just one," Austin said.

"Awesome," Ruben said.

Rubbing his arm where Nina had jabbed him, Austin stood and extended his hand to her. "Will you join me?"

Nina smiled. "I've come this far, haven't I?"

Grinning, Austin escorted her over to the hammock. They both attempted to slip into the net, but instead of finding a comfortable seat, they slipped off and went crashing to the ground.

Everyone laughed.

"Go figure," LeeAnn whispered to Zach. "We didn't even need to bring the hammock."

"I'm glad you did." He kissed her cheek. "Maybe we can set it up in the woods tomorrow and get a little alone time together?"

She bit her lip. "That sounds good."

Austin looked at Nina, dusted himself off, and shrugged. "I guess back by the fire is probably the safest place for us."

"I'd say so." Ruben chuckled, then looked at LeeAnn and Zach. "Well? The new blood always gets to pick. What'll it be?"

LeeAnn looked at Zach.

"I'm easy, babe," he said. "Pick whatever you want."

"How about vodka?" LeeAnn said. "That way, we can have fun and still keep the calories low."

"You can't go wrong with vodka," Ruben said, turning and winking at Gen and Whitney. "Girls, can you go fix us up some shots, please?"

"Sure thing," Whitney said, heading to the cabin with Gen.

LeeAnn watched as Ruben turned his attention to Milk. She sat close to the fire, tossing around the hot coals with the square side of her pie cooker. The iron end of the device was the same size as a piece of bread. LeeAnn had watched Milk load it up with the sweet ingredients, envious of the dessert but still a little too shy to ask if she could make one.

A few drinks will help loosen me up, LeeAnn thought. *Everyone here is cool anyway. Stop overthinking stuff.*

"You've been pretty quiet," Ruben said to Milk. "What are you cooking?"

"It's a raspberry and fluff pie," Milk said.

Ruben licked his lips. "Mmmm . . . that sounds pretty good. So, what are you most looking forward to about this trip?"

She stared into the bright red coals. "The peace and quiet, I suppose."

"I hear that." Ruben got out of his chair and sat down beside Milk. He sipped his beer and caressed her hair with the other hand. "The peace and quiet out here is so relaxing. Do you feel relaxed?"

Milk turned toward him but leaned away from Ruben's touch. "There was one thing I wanted to ask you about."

LeeAnn didn't understand why Milk wanted to avoid Ruben's touch. His voice was so hypnotic, and he was easily the sexiest man there. While she still had some reservations about hooking up with other people, she would've loved for Ruben to touch her like that.

"Ask away," he said.

"I thought someone mentioned that there was water here?" Milk asked. "I love swimming, and it seems like the weather's gonna be perfect."

"Oh, certainly," Ruben said. "There's a path on the side of the cabin, right near where the cars are parked. It's only about a five-minute walk, and it leads you right to it."

"What?!" Nina said. "I wish I brought my bathing suit."

Ruben shrugged. "Well, worst-case scenario, you've always got your birthday suit."

Everyone laughed as Whitney and Gen appeared, each holding a tray. Whitney approached Zach and LeeAnn, who each scooped up a shot glass, while Gen set her tray on the other side of the fire. Moving on to Austin and Nina, Whitney gave them each a shot. They thanked her and looked at Ruben. Gen handed Ruben one of her glasses and took one for herself.

"Milk," Whitney said. "This last one's for you."

"Oh . . . I'm sorry," Milk said. "I-I should've said something. I can't drink alcohol."

Gen furrowed her brow. "Why the hell not?"

"Um . . . it's—"

"Hey, relax," Ruben said. "She said she can't drink it. No need to pressure her."

Whitney walked over to the table and set her tray with the lone remaining drink, and Gen handed her a shot from her tray.

"Okay." Ruben lifted his glass. "To new experiences, and old friends."

"Cheers," several of them said.

LeeAnn threw her drink back and chased it with her beer. Her heart had been racing since they'd started hanging out by the fire and drinking. The sexual tension in the house was through the roof. It felt like with each drink that LeeAnn took, she wanted Ruben even more. There was a dark feeling of temptation swirling inside her, but she couldn't help but feel like something about the whole situation was wrong.

Can I really do this? she thought.

She looked over at Zach, examining his expression. She knew him better than anyone on the planet. The grin on his face was supposed to project delight—like he was having the time of his life—but she could see the subtleties. The insincerity was obvious to her. It was like he was wearing a mask of joy, but the true pain underneath couldn't be hidden. Not from her, at least.

It was then that it hit her like a brick to the head.

This is . . . hurting him. I'm hurting him. He just doesn't wanna admit it.

The elation from the drinks and the excitement slowly drained out of her. LeeAnn knew alcohol always tended to make her more emotional, but emotional or not, when Zach hung his head, she could see the damage to his soul as clear as day.

"Baby, is everything all right?" she whispered.

"I . . . I don't know," Zach said.

She moved in closer and pulled his ear toward her lips. "I didn't ever mean to hurt you."

Zach blinked several times, staring into the fire.

"If I told you I was only planning on fucking you this weekend, would that make you feel better?" LeeAnn asked.

"I feel weird," Zach said.

LeeAnn grabbed the side of her head, noticing that Zach's face looked suddenly blurry. She turned back to the rest of the group. Shifting her weight to one knee, she tried to stand up but fell over on her side.

"I th-think . . . I'm drunk," she said.

On her side, she could see the grin form on Ruben's face. "There's always at least one who can't handle their liquor."

HORSE
PLAY

DIRTY GAMES

When Zach finally opened his eyes, the sun was already coming up. His brain hurt in a way he'd never known was possible. He felt weak, and his stomach ached. Despite the horrific hangover, he forced himself to sit up.

"Fuck . . . How much did we drink?" he asked.

LeeAnn moaned and turned toward him. She squinted, her eyes still adjusting to the light.

"What the hell happened?" she asked.

Zach's heart started to beat faster. "I don't know . . . I— I can't remember anything."

"Me either." LeeAnn looked at the window and then back to him. "Babe—ew . . . What's that on your face?"

"Huh?" Zach mumbled, grabbing at his cheek.

"No, the other side."

She used her fingernail to scrape around his lips. Flakes of white crust fell onto the comforter.

"What is it?" he asked nervously.

LeeAnn looked closer. "I don't know . . . drool, maybe?"

"I-I'm gonna take a shower," he said.

"Okay." LeeAnn's head dropped back onto her pillow. "Wake me up when you're finished and I'll go after you."

"Right," Zach said.

As he headed into the bathroom, a feeling of dread slowly came over him. The fact that he had no recollection of anything that happened last night deeply bothered him. He wasn't the kind of guy who got hammered and figured shit out the next morning.

I don't even remember drinking that much, he thought.

As Zach turned on the hot water and reached for the soap, he noticed a salty, almost bitter taste resonating through his tastebuds.

Ugh . . . What the fuck?

He opened his mouth and vomited, letting the water rinse it out.

***

When they got downstairs, Zach noticed that everyone looked pretty hungover. But some looked worse off than others. Nina and Austin appeared every bit as destroyed as Zach and LeeAnn felt. While Ruben, Whitney, and Gen all looked like they were dealing with some repercussions, it wasn't the same kind of agony he saw on Austin and Nina's faces.

Milk was clearly the smart one. She'd avoided the drink entirely, and because of her intelligent decision, she seemed to be pain free. Still, despite appearing sober, the girl looked uncomfortable, like there was something bothering her that she didn't want to say.

But the thing that stuck out the most to Zach wasn't the varying degrees of sluggishness in their cabinmates. It was the man standing near the door who Zach had never seen before.

"Okay, Louis," Ruben said. "It was good seeing you again, my friend. You've got the tape, right?"

The man had a pencil mustache and a gummy grin. He looked like the human incarnation of a weasel. He held up a VHS tape in a sleeve and tipped his baseball cap, which read KING LOUIE.

"You know it," Louis said. "I can't wait to have a watch. And don't worry." He tapped the tape. "I'll keep it nice and safe."

"Right on," Ruben said, shifting his focus to Zach and LeeAnn. "I'll be in touch."

The door closed, and a car outside started up.

"So . . . you two had quite the night," Ruben said.

Zach's heart started to race again. "Yeah . . . I guess we had a little too much to drink."

"Have a seat," Ruben said, pointing to the couch across from him.

They both took a seat on the long sectional sofa beside Nina and Austin.

"I'd say that's an understatement," Ruben said, reaching for the remote and turning on the TV.

When he pressed play, Zach's heart fell into his stomach. Onscreen was the very couch they were sitting on. Zach saw himself. He was smiling and biting his lip, wearing a sleeping mask and a T-shirt but no pants. A massive grin stretched across his face as he let out a coo of delight.

Austin was hunched over in front of him, sucking his cock. While he took Zach into his mouth, he stroked his own shaft, growing more aroused by the second.

Beside them, on the couch, were LeeAnn and Nina. They were sixty-nining, and the delight on LeeAnn's face glowed as she ate Nina's pussy and asshole.

It was dead silent in the cabin.

As the Austin on the TV started to moan and quickly stood up, Zach felt like he might be sick. When the older man's cumshot dribbled out of the head of his cock and all over the side of Zach's face, the salty taste that he'd washed out of his mouth in the shower returned.

"W-w-what the fuck is this?!" Zach asked.

He could see the horror on LeeAnn's face, and it somehow trumped his own. She was speechless.

"This is just four consenting adults having some fun," Ruben said. "You guys got a little loose last night and did some experimenting."

"So you—you fucking filmed it?" Zach yelled.

"Actually, Gen did. You know how she just *loves* documenting."

"I didn't fucking agree to that!" Austin said. "None of us agreed to that! Give me that goddamn tape!" He got up and ripped it out of the VCR.

"What the hell is going on?" LeeAnn whispered.

"I'll . . . I'll figure it out," Zach said, still coming to grips with what he'd seen himself participating in.

"Listen, you can have the tape," Ruben said. "That won't make a difference. Louis already left with a copy. He's going to hold on to it for safekeeping."

"What the fuck is this about?!" Zach yelled, standing up.

"Money, of course," Ruben said, sounding almost shocked that he'd asked. "Isn't everything?"

Zach lifted Ruben out of his chair by the collar of his shirt. "I'm gonna fuck your world up. You're gonna be—"

Ripping free of his grasp, Ruben let out a laugh. "I'm afraid it doesn't work that way. You lay one finger on me, and I'll make sure the people closest to you see this new side of you. I'll show it to your mother, your friends, your coworkers—I'll make sure every goddamn person knows that tough-guy shit is all an act. And how, deep down . . ." Ruben grinned. "You're just a faggot at heart."

The rage boiling inside of Zach was replaced by terror. His sensitivity was bad before, but it was unmanageable now. The embarrassment that making good on such a threat could cause was irreparable.

"And speaking of coworkers . . ." Ruben turned to Nina and Austin. "I wonder what the school board would think about the principal of their middle school and a fellow member of the faculty partaking in this kind of activity. I can't imagine it would go over too well."

Zach looked back at LeeAnn. She was still in shock. Nina seemed to be coming out of it. The scowl on her face flared with anger.

"You piece of shit," Nina said. "This is blackmail!"

"Wow, someone finally figured it out," Ruben said, clapping his hands and grinning. "You know, you're smarter than you look."

"I knew I felt more than drunk last night," Nina said, eyes lighting with fury. "It felt just like that time in college when a creep spiked my drink. You fucking drugged us, didn't you?"

Gen laughed, and Whitney stood by with a stoic expression on her face.

"Wow, you figured us out, college girl," Whitney said, starting to clap.

Ruben's grin flatlined as he shook his head. He glared at Whitney but didn't say anything.

The charm and polished words that had seemed like Ruben, Whitney, and Gen's natural personas had melted away. Zach took notice of the shift, particularly with Ruben. There was a different side of him that he'd kept hidden underneath. And like a snake shedding its skin, he was finally showing himself for what he was—a heartless, money-hungry bastard.

"Fuck you!" Nina screamed.

"If you play your cards right, maybe," Ruben said.

"We didn't consent to this," Austin said.

"Yeah, well, you don't remember last night too well, though," Ruben said. "But I've got a lot of other people who say you did. Right, girls?"

Gen and Whitney both nodded in agreement.

"Milk saw it too." He turned to Milk. "Didn't you?"

A moment of awkward silence crept up until the girl's fear seemed to force her into compliance.

"Y-yeah . . ." Milk said, almost ashamed.

Ruben turned to Zach and Austin. "Besides, it was you all who were acting freaky with each other. That consent shit is between the four of you—"

A loud pounding on the door made everyone freeze.

"What the fuck is that?" Ruben asked.

Whitney looked out the window. "Some dude in a cowboy hat . . ."

"We'll discuss our business after I deal with this," Ruben said, approaching the door.

When he turned the handle, a tall man in a cowboy hat pushed his way inside. He knocked Ruben back and pointed his pistol at him.

"W-Wayne?" Milk mumbled.

He didn't pay her any attention. His eyes were filled with rage. "Give me your car keys," Wayne growled. "Each and every goddamn one of you!"

BUZZING AROUND

"Is this shit good?" Toby asked.

Gus looked down at the ounce of weed he'd dropped on the passenger seat of Toby's US Park Ranger vehicle and shook his head.

"Yeah . . . it's actually almost a little too good," Gus said.

Toby noticed the strange grimace of fear on Gus's face. Almost as if he was remembering something that made him uncomfortable.

"*Too* good?" Toby asked. "What the hell's that supposed to mean?"

"It means make sure you ain't got anywhere to go before you smoke it."

Toby squinted at it. "Why's it look so . . . yellow?"

"I ain't got all fucking day. You want it, or not? If you made me drive all the way out here for nothing, it'll be the last time I ever—"

"Of course I'll take it." Waggling his eyebrows with intrigue, Toby handed him the money and took the weed. "I'm not a fucking pussy."

Gus pocketed the money and tapped his hand against the SUV. "Either way, make sure your day's squared away before you start in with that shit."

"All right, man." Toby nodded. "Until next time."

Gus hopped into his Camaro and peeled out with Billy Squier pumping out the speakers. As Toby watched the car disappear down the road, he retrieved the joint papers from his console.

"Don't fucking tell me how to smoke," he grumbled to himself. "This ain't my first rodeo."

He rolled up a quick joint and lit it up. When he inhaled, an extreme synthetic flavor dominated his tastebuds. He took several more hits, and the strange flavor intensified. Toby's tongue and head started to feel like they were throbbing.

Why's it taste so much like . . . chemicals? he wondered.

The many colors around him slowly started to transition. When he gazed out the window of his car, Toby felt more like he was looking through a kaleidoscope than examining nature. The textures of the trees grew more wavy and sur-real. Some of their barks looked like they were melting.

Oh, no . . . Been down this path before.

Toby put the weed in the console and flicked the rest of the joint out the window.

As he looked down the stretch of forest road, he heard the roar of an engine. A car zipped past, only to screech to a halt just ahead of him. A man with a pencil-thin mustache wearing a baseball cap that read KING LOUIE jumped out of the car. He ran in Toby's direction but wasn't focused on him. The man flailed his arms around and shook his body.

"Hey, man," Toby said, sticking his head out the window. "What's going on?"

"A damn wasp flew in my window while I was driving!" the man yelled.

When Toby focused on the man's eyes, they grew black and wide like the winged creature he'd just mentioned.

"You allergic or s-something?"

"No, I just hate fucking wasps!" the man yelled, still trembling.

Toby watched the man's head shake as black antennas wormed their way through his sweaty skin.

"Holy shit," Toby whispered.

"What?" the man asked.

The wasp-like features were far more pronounced now. Yellows, blacks, and browns oozed off the man's face as Toby looked on in terror at the insectoid features gaining more detail.

"Are . . . are you gonna be all right?" Toby asked.

"Yeah, I think it's gone."

"Hey, cock breath," the radio crackled.

Toby looked over at the receiver.

"Where the fuck are you?" Jared asked. *"You said you'd be back in five."*

Toby gazed at his watch, but the numbers and hands looked a mess—like they'd all been detached and tossed into a pool of water, left to float around with each other.

"Um . . ." Toby said to himself, suddenly overwhelmed by the situation.

"Hey, fuckhead!" Jared yelled. *"Answer me!"*

Toby picked up the walkie-talkie and pressed the button.

"Yeah, I—I'm en route," he said, staring in horror at the man with the melting wasp face.

"Do I got something in my teeth or something?" the man asked.

"Well, hurry the hell up," Jared said. *"We were supposed to do a welfare check on that private campground already."*

"Huh?"

"I told you earlier when the job came in. We've gotta check out Camp Hawk. That family, the Nettles—ah, why do I even bother?"

Toby looked away from the wasp man, doing his best to ignore the insanity, and pressed the button again. His eyes were so wide that they felt like they might fall out of his skull. "Dude, seriously, what the fuck are you talking about?"

"I'm talking about how your dumb, slow ass is making us look bad! Get the fuck back here pronto, or I promise you'll regret it. Over."

Toby continued to ignore the wasp man's unsettling presence and focused on Jared's words. While he wasn't fully confident that he'd be able to drive, he turned the key in the ignition anyway.

"I've gotta get going," Toby said. "You . . . you're good, though, right?"

The insect fangs pushing out of the man's face oozed with yellow slime.

"Yeah, it's gone now," he said again.

Toby immediately stepped on the gas and took off down the road. Paranoia surging, he adjusted the rearview mirror. The wasp man was standing stoically in the middle of the road, watching him drive off, when out of nowhere, a massive insect descended upon him. Its hauntingly hairy legs wrapped around the wasp man in an instant and lifted him off the ground.

Confusion twisted around in Toby's brain. A new puzzle was on his mind as he turned his attention to the quivering road in front of him.

"He said a wasp was chasing him," Toby whispered to himself, wiping the sweat off his face. "But that looked more like a fucking horsefly . . ."

***

Bbbbbzzzzzzzzzzzzzzz.

The sound of her wings flapping was deafening. As the man in the KING LOUIE hat squirmed in the clutches of the horsefly's legs, she grew angrier.

The horsefly had always had a profound bloodlust. The urge to feed was nothing new—she was always willing to do anything to get her hands on the juice inside of the lifeforms around her. But ever since the men in the lab had held her captive, something was different.

Maybe that was when she'd been touched.

Because while imprisoned inside that transparent tank, things had changed. It wasn't just about bloodmeals any longer. It was about rage. It was about addiction. She'd already had her fill of blood, but it didn't matter. It felt like she'd been rewired.

Bzzzz-buuuuurrrrr-bzzzzzt, she thought.

She wanted to cut them. She wanted to kill them. She wanted to get drunk off their blood, even when there was no more room in her gullet. She wanted to inflict pain on every other species around her.

As the horsefly made her way toward the rocks, the man continued to cry. She loosened her grip on him and watched the man fall. After the long drop, when he smacked against the jagged rocks, she watched his blood splatter around. A feeling of anger bubbled inside her, but she still didn't know why.

Zipping down toward him, she mounted his mangled body. The gaping wound on his head caused some of his brain tissue to throb in and out the back of his broken skull. The horsefly plunged her saw-like mandibles into the quaking hole and started to lap up the excess of warm blood.

Bzzzz-mmmmm-hhhhhh.

The warm fluid tasted like heaven. The iron flavor only served to further galvanize her bottomless fury.

But she'd already inflated her body with the blood of several large animals the prior evening, and her all-night binge made her current prey a victim of violence for the sake of violence. Since she'd been held captive in the lab, that was just the way her mind worked.

As she forced herself to ingest the new blood, her body told her that it wouldn't be possible. A massive wad of congealed, crimson vomit exploded from her jowls, covering the man's ghostly complexion and gumming up the wound in his brain.

She stared away from the dying man for a moment, trying to clear her mind. A loose boulder spattered with his blood lay beside the man's body. The rock, about the size of a football, didn't distract her for long. Within seconds the rage had returned.

The idea that she couldn't eat more angered her. The horsefly turned back to the gory man and guided her mouth-saw from his neck all the way down to his belly. The spiny edges tore through his organs while piss saturated the front of his pants.

FARM OF HORRORS

"So, who did it?" Wayne asked.

As the warm breeze pushed against Milk's hair, the gun in his hand made her tremble. From her brief interaction with Wayne, she understood him to be a no-nonsense kind of fella. She was all too familiar with that type. But as Milk looked over the fence at Wayne's pasture along with her cabinmates, it wasn't hard to see why the man was so infuriated. The lively horses she'd enjoyed watching graze just the prior afternoon were all dead.

"Who fucking did it?!" Wayne pointed the gun at Ruben. "Someone's gonna talk. You're gonna tell me what happened."

The horses looked like bags of skin and bones. Like they'd been strategically deflated and bled out.

Tell me what happened . . . his voice—the voice she was running from—echoed in Milk's head again. Her ex's voice had been with her since she'd started her journey, and she had a feeling he might be staying with her indefinitely.

As her eyes zeroed in on the barrel of Wayne's gun, Milk recalled the wretched memory. When she'd woken up to his question that was only intensified by the rumble of anger in his tone. Hearing the pistol cock while slowly realizing the pressure against her stomach was the barrel pressing against it.

I told you to get rid of it, Darrel said. *If you won't . . . then I will.*

She never did get to figure out why Darrel hated her so much. He'd seemed so sweet at first. Not that the behavior was justified in any way, but Milk couldn't help but wonder if she'd done something to trigger it.

Was it me getting pregnant? she wondered. *But he's the one who got me that way. He knew we weren't using protection.*

"You better fucking talk," Wayne growled.

"Man, we didn't have shit to do with this!" Ruben said.

Wayne pulled back the hammer. "Lie to me again, asshole. See what happens."

Ruben scoffed. "You don't scare me. This ain't the first time I had a gun in my face."

Wayne kept his glare steady on him. "But it might be the last."

Milk forced herself to stop thinking about Darrel and focus on the chaos unfolding. "Wayne, y-you've got every right to be pissed. As a woman with great respect for animals and nature, I swear to you, I didn't see anyone in the house hurt your horses."

"You sleep with your eyes open?" Wayne asked.

She didn't respond.

"That's what I thought," he continued. "So this is how it's gonna go. You all are gonna tell Milk where your car keys are. She's gonna go inside and retrieve them for me, and I'll hold on to them while I hike up to the ranger tower. Once we get to the bottom of this, if you didn't have anything to do with killing my horses, your keys will be returned to you. But until then, no one's going anywhere."

"Wait, you can't just leave us stranded out here," Zach said. "We—"

"Like hell I can't," Wayne said.

"Why don't you just let one of us drive you there," Austin said, glaring at Ruben. "There's a separate issue that we might need to talk to them about anyway."

"I'm calling the shots, and I don't need any suggestions," Wayne said.

LeeAnn raised a shaking hand. "But wouldn't it be faster to drive than w—"

"It's only about a twenty-minute hike," Wayne said. "With the way these winding roads were built, the drive would actually be longer. Not that I need to keep explaining myself to the cocksuckers who killed my horses."

"We didn't do anything!" Gen said. "This is bullshit!"

"No, waking up to your entire stable annihilated is fucking bullshit!" Wayne yelled. Milk watched as Wayne's eyes glossed over. He looked deep in thought, wiping at his eye as he sniffled. "What you did to . . . to my Sweat Cream . . ." He clenched his teeth and shook his head. "You're goddamn lucky I haven't unloaded this thing already!"

Milk had seen firsthand how much Wayne adored the beautiful white horse. As her eyes darted to the blood-stained, deflated carcass in the field, she felt even more uneasy.

"Now bring me each and every one of those keys before I decide to forget about the authorities and do my own interrogating. And I promise you that I ain't gonna be as nice as they'll be."

Milk nodded. "O-okay."

The tears in Wayne's eyes had dried, replaced by a newfound fire. "Make it quick."

MOMENT OF DREAD

"You're a real dumb bitch, aren't you?" Ruben asked.

The sun beat down on Ruben and the rest of the group as they stood in front of the cabin. His anger wasn't solely because of Milk handing over their keys to the cowboy. While he would never admit it out loud, Ruben didn't like being told what to do.

Wayne had found a way to control him and his entire flock. Ruben had worked too hard, carefully orchestrating each move over many months like a chess master to successfully convince everyone to meet in that cabin. He'd put in too much work and time into the scheme for another man to come in—even if it was temporarily—and emasculate him.

"He doesn't even know how many sets of keys there were between us," Ruben continued. "But you gave him everything! Even the spares!"

"What's it matter?" Milk asked. "None of us did anything."

"How do you know that?" Whitney asked.

The group turned to her, intrigued by her question.

"These four," she continued, pointing at Zach, LeeAnn, Austin, and Nina. "They don't even remember fucking each other. Who's to say that there's some other things they don't remember doing?"

"First you try to extort us, and now you wanna blame us for the fucking horses!" Austin said.

"I don't see it that way," Gen said. "I know the four of us"—she gestured to herself, Whitney, Ruben, and Milk—"can all be accounted for. But after your kinky time, we have no idea what you all got into last night."

"Fuck you, bitch," Nina said, pushing Gen.

"Get your hands off her!" Whitney yelled.

"Everybody stop!" Ruben yelled.

They all froze.

"Let's not all start blaming each other," Ruben continued. "If we stick together, we're stronger."

Zach clenched his fist and scoffed. "Stick together? Listen to this fucking guy."

"I should knock you out right now," Austin growled. "You're a liar and a smartass."

"I wish you would try, Mr. Principal," Ruben said. "I've beaten up as many faggots over the years as you've beat off."

Austin raised his arm, preparing to throw what would've most certainly been a pathetic punch. But as his arm shot forward, a loud buzzing noise rapidly descended upon them.

The horsefly was enormous. It flew toward the group with blinding speed. The sheer scope of the creature's mandibles was impossible to miss—they looked like a pair of chainsaws made of insectoid bone and tissue.

The sawtooth connected with Austin's forearm, just below his elbow joint.

As the gushing limb fell to the floor of dead pine needles, the group screamed and ran for the cabin. Austin fell to his knees, staring down at his twitching extremity in shock, and Nina forced herself to stop.

"Austin, get up," she cried, taking hold of his good arm. But when she tried to guide him back to the door, he fell forward. He already looked so pale. "Get up!" she begged.

He was too devastated to listen. Nina tugged at his arm helplessly until the haunting hum of the horsefly's wings suddenly returned.

"Close the fucking door!" Ruben said, pushing Zach and LeeAnn out of the way.

"What the fuck *is* that thing?!" LeeAnn cried.

"I don't know!" Zach yelled. "But w-we can't just leave them out there with it."

"Screw them," Ruben said, taking hold of the doorknob. "I'm not letting that thing—"

Before he could get the door closed, Zach's fists flashed and hit him in the ear and back of the head with a two-piece, causing Ruben to fall to the floor.

"*I'll* say when the door gets closed," Zach said, turning his attention back to Nina and Austin.

Nina looked on in horror as the horsefly mounted Austin's back and plunged its sawtooth into the back of his head. As his arm was ripped from her grasp, Austin's confused screams instantly stopped and his eyes rolled up in his head. The horsefly's serrated mouth-swords vibrated like a jackhammer as it excitedly lapped up the blood.

"Baby!" Nina cried, bending over and tugging on his arm, somehow fearless in the face of the beast.

"Nina!" LeeAnn yelled. "Come back inside! Y-you can't help him anymore!"

Before another word could be said, a mass of fresh blood was regurgitated by the horsefly. Splattering in every direction, a line of vomitous crimson painted Nina's face and clothing. Hands on her face, trying to wipe the blood away, she let go of her love's hand, turned, and started to run. But the gore in her eyes sent her into the side of the cabin rather than through its door.

As her bloody, unconscious body hit the ground, Zach stepped outside and grabbed ahold of Nina. The horsefly continued to gorge and puke on Austin's lifeless body and slurp up its own vomit as Zach pulled her inside.

Once they were all inside the cabin, LeeAnn slammed the door and locked it.

ODD OBSERVATIONS

"Did you shoot someone?" Jared asked.

Wayne furrowed his brow. "No . . . even though I probably should've."

Jared looked back through the scope, squinting at what appeared to be a massive puddle of blood in front of the cabin. "I thought you said the bodies of the horses were all still on the pasture?"

"That's right," Wayne said.

Jared whipped around and pointed his rifle at Wayne.

"What the hell are you doing?" Wayne asked, putting his hands up.

"What you're telling me and what I'm seeing ain't matching up."

Jared glanced at Toby, who stood hunched over a small table. He had his face an inch away from the half of his peanut butter and jelly sandwich that had been removed from his Ziplock.

"Toby, look alive!" Jared yelled.

Toby shrieked before looking up at his partner.

"Take his firearm and bag it until we can determine exactly what happened down there."

"This is bullshit—I came to you!" Wayne yelled.

Jared had noticed his partner was a little off since he'd returned from his drive. Normally, Toby was always high and giggling. But today was different. He seemed more serious, like he was legitimately upset about something. Jared had already asked him several times if he was all right, but Toby's shaky nods hadn't convinced him.

"You'll shut your goddamn mouth," Jared said. "We're the ones conducting the investigation. You'll get your gun back just as soon as we get this situation squared aw— Toby, what the fuck are you doing?!"

He looked back at Jared blankly, unable to realize the error of his ways.

Jared huffed in annoyance. "I didn't mean your damn *sandwich* bag, dummy. I meant a clean bag—you know, like to preserve evidence and stuff."

When Toby looked down at the PB&J sandwich smashed into Wayne's gun, he didn't seem sure how to remediate the situation.

"I'll . . . I'll take care of it," Toby whispered, slipping the bagged gun into his travel backpack.

Jared shook his head in disappointment, but his eye stopped on the corkboard.

"Aw, shit," he mumbled.

"What is it?" Toby asked.

The note read: *Welfare check on Camp Hawk—Mason Nettles and family.*

"It's shocking how little you care about this fucking job," Jared said. "I radioed you earlier. We're supposed to do a welfare check at Camp Hawk!"

Wayne raised his eyebrow. "Camp Hawk? Why?"

Jared curled his lip, almost offended that he would ask. "It's official ranger business."

"That place is close to my property," Wayne said, furrowing his brow. "If something's happening over there, I have a right to know. Maybe it's connected to what happened on my pasture."

"C-C-Camp Hawk?" Toby's eyes were filled with terror.

"All right, relax, cowboy," Jared said. "It's nothing much, they're just wanting us to do a welfare check."

"But why?" Wayne asked.

Jared sucked his teeth, growing annoyed with the questions. "Because I guess this stupid family isn't back from their trip yet. So they just want someone to head over and check it out."

"Hmm . . ." Wayne grumbled, seemingly concocting his own theories in his head. "That's strange."

"Well . . . shouldn't we check it out then?" Toby asked.

"If your ass had been here on time, we'd have already checked it out," Jared said. "But we now have a more pressing matter at hand. Wayne here is our top priority right now." He looked down at the tower's ladder and gestured to the cowboy with his gun. "We've wasted enough time. We'd better get going."

HOLDING DOWN THE FORT

"You put your fucking hands on me again and you're dead!" Ruben yelled. "You hear me?!"

Zach was so pissed off at Ruben that he was having trouble controlling his emotions. The ruthless boxer that took out his problems on his opponents' faces had returned. He was snapping into fight mode. The manipulative man had humiliated not only him but LeeAnn as well. Zach had more than a bone to pick with him.

"Let's get one thing straight," Zach said, glaring at Ruben from across the room. "I'm not scared of you. If you got some kind of problem, we can handle it right here."

"You asked for it." Ruben pulled a switchblade from his pocket and ejected the knife.

"I'll take that fucking thing and stick it up your ass!" Zach yelled.

"That sounds like something *you'd* be more into," Ruben fired back.

"You guys!" Whitney yelled. "We can't be fighting each other! How are you not focused on that fucking thing outside?! W-what are we gonna do?"

"I know what we're doing," Zach said, picking up Nina. "We're going to wait in our room for the rangers to get back. Alone."

LeeAnn stayed quiet, following Zach to the stairs.

"Um . . . it might be better if we stick together," Milk said. "Don't you think?"

Zach paused at the bottom of the steps, looking down at Nina's unconscious body. Flashbacks of the videotape flickered in his mind.

Austin's face in his crotch.

Nina's ass riding LeeAnn's mouth.

The words LeeAnn had said near the bonfire—just before things got hazy—echoed in his head.

If I told you that I was only planning on fucking you this weekend, would that make you feel better?

At the time, had the drug cocktail not taken effect so quickly, he would've said yes. He would have jumped for joy. But they'd been robbed of that organic moment. Whether LeeAnn was willing to sacrifice her own desires to avoid hurting him or not was no longer relevant after the acts they'd participated in the prior evening.

Everything is so fucked-up, Zach thought.

Zach looked at Ruben and his girls with disgust, finally ready to answer Milk's question. "Normally, sticking together would make the most sense. But you aren't normal people. You're evil, fucked-up people. We're better off without you."

"That shit you did was your own choice," Gen said. "Don't get mad at us because you—"

"Just stay the fuck away from us!" LeeAnn yelled. She looked back at Zach, who had a death stare aimed directly at Ruben. "C'mon, babe. Let's go."

As they made their way up the stairs, they could hear the rest of the group grumbling. But Zach didn't care what they were saying. He was only concerned with keeping LeeAnn safe.

"Wha . . . what's going on?" Nina whispered.

Zach looked down at her. The massive, egg-shaped bump on her forehead from running into the cabin continued to rise. A little bit of dried blood was crusted over the cut area along with the splatter of the creature's regurgitation. Despite Nina having screwed around with his woman, he felt pity for her. They'd all been tricked.

"We're going into our room," Zach said.

"Austin?" Nina mumbled. "Why are you carrying me?"

He entered the room and sat Nina down on the bed.

"You hit your head," Zach said. "You were out for a few minutes."

When LeeAnn approached Zach, he could tell the pain on her face was in anticipation of having to remind Nina what had happened outside.

"I feel dizzy," Nina said.

"Just lay back for a second and relax," LeeAnn said.

She guided her back, then turned to Zach and gestured toward the corner of the room. Once they were far enough away from Nina, LeeAnn whispered in his ear.

"Maybe we shouldn't tell her . . ."

Zach shook his head. "She's going to find out one way or another."

"But I don't know if she can handle it right now. Sh—"

The sliding glass door beside them suddenly shattered. Austin's lifeless body crashed through the balcony entrance and pulled down the blinds that were drawn on one side of the door. His pulverized head smacked against the floor. With fresh gashes from the glass shards now covering his body in addition to missing an arm from the horsefly attack, he was a bloody glob of mutilation.

Nina and LeeAnn shrieked in unison at the sound of the flapping wings of the horsefly.

"Ruuuuuuuuuunn!" Zach yelled, pushing the girls toward the door.

As the beast made its way inside through the broken balcony entrance, the girls rushed out the door. Zach glanced back, watching the horsefly buzz toward him in a swift blur.

He was barely able to slip into the hallway and get the door closed in time. But just as it settled in its frame, the creature's saw-fangs penetrated the wooden door.

The horsefly's mandibles hit the door with such force that a wood fragment splintered out, slashing the side of Zach's bicep.

"Shit!" he yelled, grabbing his arm. "Keep running! It's coming through the fucking door!"

As Zach, LeeAnn, and Nina made their way to the stairs, the buzzing drew closer.

"What the fuck is going on up there?" Ruben yelled from downstairs.

"It's inside!" LeeAnn shrieked.

The upstairs bathroom door opened.

"What the hell is going o—"

Gen's question was suddenly interrupted by the horsefly's sword-like mouth. It rammed the serrated edge into her chest, leaving a massive, jagged puncture wound above her heart.

The force of the stab sent Gen toppling sideways over the banister, the power of the beast launching her far enough that she landed with an unforgiving thud on the island in the kitchen. When her body hit, a generous amount of blood splattered all over the counter and surrounding area.

"W-we gotta get the fuck outta here!" Ruben said, pulling open the front door. "That thing's a killer!"

Tears of terror were already streaking down Whitney's face. She kept her eyes on the hovering creature while replying to Ruben. "Where we gonna go?!"

"Anywhere but here—the fucking cowboy's house!"

"But Gen needs our help!"

The horsefly swooped down and mounted Gen's quivering body, using its mouth like a chainsaw to carve through her bones like a slasher in a horror movie.

"Then *you* fuckin' help her," Ruben said, angrily huffing his way out the door.

The sadistic bug finished sawing through Gen's neck, sending her head plopping onto the floor. A stream of crimson flooded from the stump. The horsefly eagerly lapped at the blood like a child with an ice cream cone on a hot day.

Whitney rushed out the front door, but Milk stayed, moving closer toward Nina and LeeAnn at the bottom of the stairs.

"Should we follow them?" LeeAnn asked, looking at the open door, then back to Zach.

Zach eyed the ajar bedroom door on the other side of the kitchen and took LeeAnn's hand. "No, follow me!"

They raced into the room, and once Nina and Milk had made it inside after them, Zach closed the door and locked it.

"Everyone quiet," Zach whispered. "Get by the window and unlock it. Upstairs, that thing carved its way right through the fucking door."

As LeeAnn flipped the window lock, Nina pressed up against the wall, emitting a whimper of horror like a traumatized puppy.

"We've gotta keep quiet," LeeAnn said.

"Keep the blinds down," Milk said. "Horseflies mainly locate their prey based on visual cues. If it can't see us or hear us, it'll probably leave once it's done feeding."

Zach glared at Milk, unsure how he felt about her being inside the room with them. He'd have preferred for her to stay with her people, but the carnage had unfolded too quickly for any debate.

They were stuck with her.

THE HIKE

"Would you hurry the fuck up already?" Jared asked.

Toby could hear the annoyance in his partner's voice. Inside the dark stall, he adjusted his backpack as he continued to vomit. While the nausea was hitting hard, on the plus side, the hallucinations were finally starting to wear off.

"I-I'm feeling kinda sick . . ." Toby yelled.

Jared huffed. "We don't have time for you to be sick! You already slowed us down enough today! Move your ass!"

"We've been standing out here forever," Wayne said. "Maybe you should just leave him behind, and you and I can go down there."

"Maybe you can just mind your goddamn business and let me do my job. That's my fucking partner in there that you're disrespecting. We don't fly solo. If shit hits the fan down there and I gotta take some of these punks out, I need my boy Toby watching my back."

As Jared rambled on, Toby started to feel like he was going to be okay. He wiped the puke from his lips and sat up and mumbled, "Fucking Gus was right. That shit is no joke."

Toby slung the backpack over his shoulder, and to his chagrin, the walkie-talkies clipped to the pack fell into the dark shithole.

"Fuck!" Toby said. "Goddamn idiot! Why didn't you just put them in the bag?"

"What the hell's going on in there?" Jared yelled. "We've gotta go, *now*! We've only got another hour until sundown, and we need to look at those horses in the light!"

"All right, all right," Toby said, finally managing to push his way out of the crapper.

"It's about damn time," Wayne said.

The three of them took to the trail, moving with urgency. They traveled through the warm woods as streaks of sunlight sliced between the shadowy trees.

"How much longer is it?" Toby asked, wiping the sweat off his forehead with his bandanna.

"How are you even a fucking forest ranger and you don't know?" Wayne asked.

"You're preaching to the choir, Wayne," Jared said. "In case you haven't noticed, Toby just kind of aims for the bare minimum. I wouldn't be surprised if he didn't know any of these trails. He's too busy fishbowling the truck."

"Hey . . . let's not start rumors with the locals, okay?" Toby said.

As they came to a fork in the path, Wayne slowed and looked at Toby. "If it was any more obvious that you were on dope, you'd be glowing green."

"Yeah," Jared laughed. "Like the Hulk or something— but without all the muscles, and a small wiener. And—"

"What the fuck is that?" Wayne asked, pointing through the trees.

Toby turned to see a massive horsefly perched on a tree branch. The very same horsefly that had snatched the wasp man up in the middle of the road. The eerie green glow that the creature emitted was visible in the darkening woods. It stared back at them, motionless.

"It was real . . ." Toby whispered.

"G-gimme my goddamn gun," Wayne commanded.

"Be quiet!" Jared said. "You don't wanna wake it up!"

"Shoot it!" Wayne said. "Or give me the gun and I'll—"

In a wink, the horsefly came to life, emitting a shrill buzz before Wayne could finish his plea. The blood-caked fly zipped by, its serrated mandible cutting through Wayne's midsection like a poop-knife through diarrhea. As his guts tumbled to the ground, Wayne's upper body flew backward, somersaulting over itself and spraying blood all over Toby and Jared.

They looked at each other and screamed.

"Fucking run!" Jared yelled.

He raised the rifle and fired several shots in the direction of the buzzing. But the horsefly moved so quickly that its position had shifted by the time the bullets left the barrel of the gun.

The beast mounted Wayne's disemboweled upper half, giving Toby a small measure of relief. As they dashed down the trail, creating distance between themselves and the murderous horsefly, he prayed that Wayne's body would be enough of a distraction for them to escape.

THE BARN

"Are you sure we should stay in here?" Whitney asked. "Don't you think the house would be a better—"

"Bitch, did I ask you to fucking think?" Ruben asked. "Not that I should have to explain myself, but the barn doesn't have any windows for that . . . that *thing* to see into or bust through." He looked at the various farm tools hung near the entrance, bypassing the pitchfork and shovel for the axe. He took it down and leaned it up against the wall. "Plus, at least in here, we have plenty of weapons."

"It just . . . it doesn't feel *safe*," Whitney whispered. "I don't like being in here."

With every word that she spoke, Ruben's blood pressure rose. He was tired of being questioned. He thought back to the cabin, where Zach had hit him with a two-piece and knocked him on his ass. When he'd regained his bearings and glanced over at the girls, Whitney in particular had this look on her face—like when those punches stunned him, they stunned her respect for him at the same time. It was a mixed frown, equal parts disgust, embarrassment, and cringe. The tough guy that had been calling the shots for her didn't look so tough anymore. He could see she doubted him now, and her doubt was the spark for his rage.

There was something else that had pissed him off inside the cabin too. After he'd played the video tape in front of the others, Nina had accused them of drugging her. They'd gone over the plan countless times, but Whitney must've tuned out for the most basic and important rule: when you drug someone, you don't tell them you did.

While he'd held his ire in, when Whitney told Nina that she'd figured them out after she made the accusation, he could've hit the roof. Normally, he would've slapped the shit out of her on the spot. But he didn't want to show their prey any weakness in the ranks. Above all else, it was about extorting Austin and his fat bankroll.

"You really feel safe here?" Whitney persisted. "Can't we just—"

"Nothing's safe right now," Ruben growled. "There's a giant fuckin' insect outside *eating* people."

Whitney grimaced in angst, stomping her foot. "Why can't you ever just listen to me? You *never* listen to me!"

"Keep your goddamn voice down!"

She kept it raised defiantly. "I told you when we were getting settled in that I had a bad feeling about this! But you didn't *listen*! And now look at us! We're alone, and no one wants to help us!"

"We don't need no one's help!"

"Speak for yourself!" Whitney's eyes lit on fire. "When shit hit the fan, Zach looked a lot more ready than you was."

Ruben took a step toward her. "No one's more fuckin' ready than me."

"Yeah? Is that why you got knocked out?"

When the words left her mouth, Ruben watched the fire in Whitney's eyes fade. The instant regret was obvious as she rushed to apologize. "I-I didn't mean—"

Ruben backhanded her with everything he had. The vicious blow sent her on her ass, and the open palm quickly turned into a closed fist.

"What the fuck did you say to me, bitch?!" Ruben yelled, slamming his fist into the side of her mouth.

Blood smeared over her face from the gash on her lip. As the next blow landed, it felt like a bit of the weight on Ruben's shoulders lessened. The thudding of knuckle against meat eased his mind, and he savored each additional shot to her head.

"Is that how you see me still?!" he yelled.

It didn't take long for Whitney's face to start to look monstrous. Her teeth were broken and knocked out; her nose was crooked and oozing blood and snot. The rising knots on her forehead and cheeks were accompanied by many gashes, one exposing a piece of her facial bones.

"Say something else!" Ruben growled.

Despite the brutality of the beating, the anger inside Ruben continued to fuel him. The fight was long over, but he wasn't done. With each strike, his hunger for the next only grew, because as he continued to pound the crimson mask, he didn't see Whitney's face anymore.

He saw Zach's.

SUCKLE OF FILTH

Bbbbbzzzzzzzzzzzzzz.

The horsefly dropped the lower half of the cowboy's carcass on the ground. It was dark near the lake, but as she looked up at the tree branches overhanging the water, the white orbs stuck to them glowed.

Bzzz-burrr-hhhmmm-bzzzt-mmm? she thought.

She remained confused as the memories of the feedings and mutilations flickered in her mind. Nothing was enough. She'd kill one but fly quickly to the next. The feeding filled her body to the seams, yet she was still famished. So hungry and at the same time so full that she'd regurgitated the blood she'd already stored.

Perching on a log sticking half out of the water, she elevated her wings and exposed her rotund body. She was like one giant, rage-filled blood bag. Clusters of normal-size horseflies keyed in on her glowing, pulsating form. They all lined up like babies would for their mother's milk, each picking out a spot to suckle from.

Hhhmmmmm-bzzz-buurrrt-bzzzzt.

The tiny, piercing fangs plunged into her body, creating a pleasureful pain. The transfer of lifeforce at hand was causing the horseflies to bustle with delight.

Bbbbbbzzzzzzzzzzt.

But as the young fed upon her, she continued to ponder the mysteries of her existence. While she wondered why she was different than the rest of her kind, she wasn't expecting the question to be answered. And when the answer suddenly manifested, she couldn't have been more shocked. There was no way for her to know whose voice it was that had responded inside her head, but an answer came nonetheless. There was only one person that it could've been.

God.

It was God who had chosen her to bring about a new way of life, to be His soldier and advance her species into the next phase of existence. It would explain why she was so much bigger than every other horsefly she'd ever seen. It would explain why she was so special and why she got inexplicable feelings, acting on them like she'd been possessed by an entity. She was enlightened.

Brrrzzz-hhmmm-buzzzrrt-zuuuum.

She thought on it more, considering that it might not be God whispering in her ear. No, that wasn't it. It *had* to be God; there was no one else it could be. She'd been chosen—it was undeniable. God wanted the others to share her rage, to taste what this new enlightenment felt like. It was the evolution of their species.

She looked up at the big white globs clinging to the trees, knowing that it was her duty to protect them.

Her thoughts were interrupted by a splash in the water. She saw nothing but her reflection. And in that reflection, she saw her huge, glowing body, and each of her tiny sisters individually lighting up like neon bulbs as they finished getting their fill.

COMMON GROUND

LeeAnn and the rest of the group had grown weary of talking about the creature. They'd been chatting fearfully for hours, their minds replaying the carnage and terror. She was tired of wondering when the horsefly might come back. She was glad things had finally calmed down and everyone was quietly taking a break. She hoped that Wayne and the forest rangers would be back soon, but with each minute that dwindled away, it felt less likely.

While LeeAnn sat in the corner of the room, in the comfort of Zach's arms, Nina lay on the bed in the fetal position. She was grateful that Nina had finally stopped crying, but LeeAnn knew another breakdown most likely wouldn't be far off. She couldn't even imagine what it would be like if she'd lost Zach in the mayhem and been thrust together with strangers while still feeling alone.

Even though Zach was still there, in another way, she *did* feel alone. As her emotions intensified, the guilt in her belly gnawed away at her until she couldn't be silent any longer.

"I . . . I can't help but feel like this is all my fault," LeeAnn whispered.

"I think you're being a little hard on yourself," Zach whispered back, stroking the side of her head.

Milk sat on the edge of the bed looking like she was doing her best to mind her business. LeeAnn still wasn't happy with her. The girl had played a part in creating the schism between the group, but exactly how big of a part was still yet to be seen.

"I mean, I shouldn't have suggested any of this," LeeAnn continued, nudging her head against his chest. "Last night, by the fire . . . I-I saw the hurt in your eyes. When I brought all this up, I thought you were curious about other people—I thought we were on the same page. And as much as that intimidated me, it gave me confidence. Reassurance that I wasn't going to hurt you. But . . . I should've known better."

"I should've explained how I felt," Zach said. "But instead, I made you play detective."

"Why didn't you? Baby, you know you can tell me anything, right?"

"When you originally suggested the idea . . . it felt like a bombshell dropped. If I had told you no, then it just would've been in the back of your head forever. You know, it's like when you tell someone they can't have something, and they want it ten times more. But I thought . . . I thought if I just went along with it, you'd maybe just get it out of your system, and then we could go back to how things were. I just wanted you to be happy. All I ever wanted to do was make you happy."

LeeAnn's bottom lip quivered as she raised her head and planted a gentle, loving kiss on him.

"Well, guess what?" she asked, feeling a tear run down her cheek.

"What?"

"You're right. After this, things are gonna go back to exactly how they were." She stroked the side of his face with her hand. "I promise you."

Zach shook his head and bit his lip. She could see him holding back the tears. "I hope so."

"I'm sorry last night happened," Milk said. She looked at Nina. "That goes for you too."

They all looked at Milk with judging eyes. None of them seemed to believe the girl. It was a convenient time for an apology, considering they were all stuck together until they figured out a plan.

"At first, nothing was really happening," Milk continued. "Just everyone getting a little tipsy and having a good time. But then I noticed that the four of you were acting much more . . . sloppy after your shots." She shifted her gaze to the wall, unable to make eye contact with them. "When they brought you inside, I thought everyone was going to bed. But I saw what they did."

"And what did they do?" LeeAnn asked.

Milk shook her head. "They set you guys up. The girls positioned you and egged you on. They manipulated you into . . . what you saw on the tape."

"And you just stood by," Zach said, disgust dripping from his words. "Didn't you? You let it happen, right?"

"It's not as simple as that," Milk said.

"Of course it is! That's why you didn't take one of the shots," LeeAnn said. "You knew they were drugging us."

"No, that's not why."

"Then why the fuck didn't you take a drink?" LeeAnn pressed.

"Because I'm pregnant, okay?" Milk said.

"She'd say anything," Nina interjected.

Milk got up from the bed and pulled a piece of paper from the inside of her bra. She quickly unfolded it and showed them the image of her sonogram.

"I'm not one of them," Milk said. "I just got caught up."

"What does that even mean?" Nina asked.

Milk huffed; her anxiety was audible. "It's a long story."

"Well, we've got plenty of time," Zach said. "None of us are going to even consider trusting you until you've explained yourself." He pointed toward Nina and then back at LeeAnn and himself. "The three of us have already been fucked over. In that way, we're bonded. For this to work, we *need* to know."

With her eyes freshly glossed over, Milk nodded. "Fair enough." She stared at the wall like it was a portal to serenity. "This wasn't my first child. My first child's dead."

The tension in everyone's judgmental looks slightly loosened, hampered by shock and sadness.

"He beat me good enough that I miscarried. I regret letting him put another baby inside me. But it wasn't like I had a choice—it wasn't like he knew how to take no for an answer. When I found out, this time I didn't tell him. It seemed like he beat me even harder when he knew I was pregnant. So I stayed quiet about this one."

Nina reached over and placed her hand on Milk's, using her thumb to slowly stroke her.

"I knew I had to get out of there—for my baby's sake. I couldn't deal with the guilt of another death on my hands. Even though I didn't do it myself, I still should've protected him." She caressed her stomach as tears continued to flow. "So, I finally got her out of there, but I had nowhere to go. Ruben was the only one who offered to take us in."

"I'm . . . I'm so sorry that you had to go through that," LeeAnn said.

"Oh, it didn't end there," Milk said. "Ruben was a really nice guy . . . at first. But once he sweet-talked me into telling him about my past, he had exactly what he wanted. He found Darrel—my baby's father. In fact, he's got him on speed dial now. He says he's just waiting for the day I step out of line, and he'll call him right up. The first time I defied him, he drove me out to Darrel's farm—where I used to live. He parked on the road and just stared at me. I cried and begged him, knowing that if he dropped me off there, I might not ever leave. That was the last time I disobeyed him . . ."

"I knew that guy was a fucking piece of shit," Zach said. "I knew it right when I met him."

"I'm sorry I didn't do anything to stop them," Milk cried. "I-I was so scared, though. I was scared for my baby."

Nina and LeeAnn both moved in and hugged her.

"We understand now," LeeAnn said.

"That's right, sweetie," Nina said. "You don't have to say anything else."

"We'll find a way out of this," LeeAnn said. "And once we're out of here, we'll help you get away from Ruben."

"O-o-okay," Milk sniffled out.

"Speaking of which, shouldn't Wayne and the rangers be back by now?" Nina asked.

"I'd say so," LeeAnn said.

Zach stood up, cracked his knuckles, and started to pace. "How long are we gonna wait? Wayne said twenty minutes, and it's been hours." He peeked out the window. "It's dark outside. Who's to say that thing didn't get them? Isn't that the most logical explanation?"

"I suppose so," LeeAnn said.

"We've got to start entertaining the idea that the cavalry isn't coming—that we might need to find a way out of here on our own."

"But Wayne took all the keys," Milk said. "I gave them to him, remember?"

Zach nodded. "Right. Well, I guess that leaves us with only two options then: we either need to find him and retrieve the keys . . ."

Nina's eyes suddenly lit up.

". . . or," Zach continued, "we have to take our chances and hike our way out of here."

"The spare!" Nina said, sitting up like a tired crackhead coming to life for a hit.

"You've got a spare?!" LeeAnn smiled for the first time since she could remember.

"Not exactly," Nina said.

The grin melted off LeeAnn's face.

"Austin . . ." The mere mention of her dead lover's name pained her. Nina clutched her heart and grimaced before finding the strength to continue. "I-I have a tendency to lock my keys in the car sometimes. He'd always make fun of me for it—told me that I called Triple A more than I called my parents."

Nina chuckled for a second, reliving the memory. It was obvious that she still hadn't come to grips with his violent demise. "Anyway . . . he put a spare in a little magnetized box under the car."

"We've got a way out of here!" LeeAnn squealed.

"But what about the others?" Milk asked.

"Once we get out of here, we can send help," Zach said.

"Yeah. Besides, who knows where they are anyway," Nina said. "When should we go?"

Zach paused in front of the girls. "It doesn't make sense for us all to go." He glanced over at LeeAnn. "I could get there quickly . . ."

LeeAnn's heart started to race. "Baby, no . . ."

"I have to," Zach said. "I'm the fastest, and there's no sense in all of us being exposed—not after seeing what that thing is capable of. After I grab the spare, I'll pull the car up to the front door, and you three can pile in. Then . . . I guess we've just gotta hope for the best."

"But when should we do it?" Nina asked.

"Maybe late tonight would be the best time," Zach said. "That thing'll be asleep."

"But horseflies don't sleep, though," Milk said. "They just rest."

Zach raised an eyebrow. "Wouldn't we be able to hear it coming with the buzzing?"

"Maybe, but there's also a possibility that she could be quietly resting on a branch nearby, and we wouldn't hear a thing. Until it's too late."

"Hmm . . . yeah, obviously that's no *normal* horsefly," Zach said.

"Correct. Her violent tendencies make me wonder *if* she even rests. She was relentless."

"She?" LeeAnn asked.

"I say 'she' because it's only the females who actually bite. They have to in order to gather the bloodmeal for their offspring."

"How do you know all this?" LeeAnn asked.

"I lived on a farm growing up, and then again with my baby's father for some time, and I became a bit of a bug nerd," Milk said. "There wasn't much else to do out there, so I got familiar with the animals and insects. They were my friends—especially when I had no one else. Well, not the horseflies. They suck. But you know what I mean."

"What does the gender matter?" Nina said. "We need to figure out when to make our move."

"Well . . . if that thing could be roaming around at any time of day, I suppose morning would make the most sense," Zach said.

LeeAnn breathed a sigh of relief.

"I would need the daylight to help me locate the key under the car anyway," Zach continued. "And getting a little rest before we leave is probably a good idea. I should be fresh for the sprint. If I cross paths with that thing, I'm going to need all the energy I can get."

A feeling of dread rumbled inside LeeAnn. She didn't want Zach to take that risk, but she knew arguing with him would be useless.

"Okay," LeeAnn said. "It's been a fucked-up day. I'm not sure if we'll be able to get much rest, but I guess we should try."

The others agreed.

She got up from the bed and took one of the spare blankets on the dresser and draped it over her and Zach as they huddled in the corner.

"You don't want the bed?" Nina asked.

"You and Milk take it," LeeAnn said. "We'll be fine."

"Thanks . . ." Nina said, still with a look of heartbreak in her eyes.

LeeAnn could plainly see the pain she was dealing with, but never would she comprehend it. Or at least that's what she hoped. But as she looked over at Zach, who was already resting his eyes, part of her knew there was a possibility that she might.

BREAKING IN

Ruben's knuckles still hurt. He sat, slumped and wide-eyed, against the wall of the barn, staring at Whitney's body. A puddle of blood surrounded her motionless head.

You didn't need her anyway, Ruben thought. *That bitch didn't respect you. All she did was doubt you. She was a liability.*

Pounding Whitney's face into the ground felt good, but that was why it had taken him so long to stop. Still, it didn't feel like it was enough. Zach was the one who'd made a fool of him—he was the one Ruben *really* wanted a piece of.

Chill out. You can't be thinking about all that with a fuckin' monster on the loose. I gotta get the fuck outta here. If the cowboy shows up again with those rangers, this ain't gonna look good.

He listed out the competing priorities in his head:

Stay clear of the killer insect.

Stay clear of the forest rangers.

Fuck-up Zach's bitch-ass.

"Fuck!" he yelled.

He could deal with a lot of things, but being bested wasn't one of them. The rage inside caused another violent outburst. He elbowed the wall of the barn behind him, attempting to release some of his frustration while giving his knuckles a rest.

As he continued to bang on the wall, he came to grips with the idea that he might have to catch up with Zach's bitch-ass after the fact. Escape was going to be the most important thing. Plus, with the way the goddamn bug was mutilating everyone in its path, maybe what he'd done to Whitney could be pinned on the horsefly.

Yeah, it was the fuckin' fly that did it to her, he reasoned.

A buzzing noise closing in near the front of the barn door drew his attention. As an eerie green glow under the wooden barrier manifested, he wondered if his tantrum had drawn the beast to him. Ruben grabbed the axe by his side and gritted his teeth.

I'll kill that motherfucker my goddamn self.

But his bravado quickly dissolved when he saw the army of tiny, illuminated horseflies swarming under the door. As the winged vampires rushed toward him, he screamed. The countless glowing bodies sprung upon him, relentless with their aggression. The pangs of pain stabbed into his face and the rest of his body, each bite causing a burning sensation to surge deep into his tissue.

He dropped his weapon and continued to scream, but the bugs just kept coming. Using his hand, he raked his fingers across the swarm, ripping some to pieces. But as he rolled on the ground, trying to protect himself, the intensity of the anguish became too much. Ruben's movements slowed, and everything faded to black.

***

Bzzz-burrr-hhhmmm-bzzzt-mmm, she thought.

The horsefly waited with anticipation on the other side of the door, listening to her prey thrash about inside. And as her adopted babies did God's work, the horsefly couldn't have been prouder. She listened to her tiny followers who had suckled upon her body—the enlightened insects chosen to carry forth the word of God—as they wreaked havoc on humanity.

The thought of the glowing chosen buzzing with angst around them, fighting to ensure their mission was a success, made her emotional. Their effort was selfless, and their intensity and grit were bottomless. The sound of their slurps as they gorged on the humans was music to her sensory receptors. They would share the wealth and enlighten that entire species too. The brave children would ensure the message branched out and increased their numbers.

They wouldn't be stopped.

Their tiny, overfed bodies began to explode from overindulgence, sounding like pop rocks touching tongue. The racket excited the horsefly. The larger vessels would be of great use. While slaughtering the humans remained her top priority, she was also tired. A couple extra pairs of hands would go a long way in her mission.

As the humans inside the barn screamed in agony, the bodies of the smaller flies continued to erupt. She knew their mission came with a cost, but the massacre still saddened her.

Burrr-bzzz-mmm-burr.

Their deaths would not be in vain or forgotten. They'd done all they could to edify the heathens who threatened their new collective future. The horsefly was grateful for the support of her children and was already thinking about how to ensure she made the most of their sacrifice.

THE SPARE KEY

"What's wrong?" Milk asked.

She was grateful the group had decided to accept her after hearing her out. It had been hard for her to share her situation with Darrel—especially after Ruben had used it against her—but she was glad that she'd decided to. At least they were all on the same page now. She hadn't expected any help from LeeAnn and Zach after everything that had happened. Even if they changed their minds and decided not to help her, she wouldn't be mad at them. She would always appreciate them even offering.

"I can't stop thinking about him," Nina said.

Milk rolled to Nina's side of the bed and put her arm around her. "I didn't know him very well, but one thing I could tell from just being around the two of you was how much he cared about you."

"I-I know we didn't love each other like that," Nina whimpered. "But we did love each other. He was only with me so the school would think he . . . you know . . . he liked women. But even though the physical part of our relationship was never there, he was always so sweet to me. He noticed the little things—like how I lock my keys in the car."

"He sounds like a great man," Milk said.

"He was." Nina nodded. "His sweetness is the reason that key is under the car—the reason we have a chance. Austin just . . . he always took care of me." She was bawling as she forced out the final words: "And more than anything, when he was in pain, I just wanted to return the favor."

Milk hugged her, feeling Nina's tears moisten her chest. She whispered, "All you can do now is what he would've wanted—get the fuck outta here."

"Yeah," Nina said. "You're right."

"I know it's hard . . . but try to be strong. For him."

"Okay."

"Is everything all right?" LeeAnn asked from their corner of the room, opening her eyes and stretching.

"I'm fine," Nina said. "Just a little emotional."

"I guess the sun is finally showing itself," Zach said, scratching the side of his face nervously. "Still no sign of Wayne or the forest rangers?"

Milk shook her head.

"Well, I guess I should probably get going, then." Zach stood up and cautiously peeked through the blinds.

LeeAnn pulled him away and hugged him. It was clear that she was trying to hold it back, but she started to sob anyway. "Y-you better come back."

"Of course I'm coming back," Zach whispered. "It'll take more than a fucking horsefly to stop me."

"You promise?"

"I've got to. We've still gotta lay in the hammock together this afternoon, right?" He grabbed her butt cheek playfully, doing his best to keep the mood light.

LeeAnn forced a giggle through her tears.

"Well, I guess it's time," Zach said.

They crept out of the bedroom, listening carefully before moving forward. The front door remained ajar, and Gen's deflated corpse still lay atop the kitchen island. She looked like a Thanksgiving turkey fit for an asylum—like she'd been carved up by a maniac. One of her bloody arms was cut down to the bone, hanging off the counter's edge by a single string of skin.

Milk groaned to herself. Revisiting the violence caused her to snap back into defense mode. Her hand rested on her belly as she thought about the child. She still hadn't named her little girl. Naming the child almost felt like jinxing it. Once she'd protected her long enough to give birth, only then would she feel entitled to name her.

"I don't see anything," Zach said, peeking through the blinds of the window. "What about you?"

LeeAnn shook her head from the other side of the room.

"Okay . . ." The fear in Zach's tone was clear. "You guys hold up near the door. When I pull that car up, just move as fast as you can." He turned to Nina. "It has power locks, right?"

She nodded.

As much as the cut-up body disgusted Milk, she had to protect her baby. She wasn't about to stand around weapon-less but wasn't sure what—if anything—would be useful against the powerful creature.

C'mon, think . . .

The creature's big eyes and buzzing wings came to mind. *I'm not gonna be able to hit its wings with anything in here . . .*

She was relieved when she spotted the fire extinguisher on top of the fridge. She remembered Ruben joking about it the prior night, by the campfire.

That might be just enough to stun it.

Zach was pacing at the door when Milk joined the others. "Anything else I should know about the car?"

"I-I don't think so," Nina said. "Oh! The key's on the frame near the rear driver's side."

"Rear driver's side." Zach took a deep breath. "Got it." He turned to LeeAnn and kissed her. When he finally pried his lips away, he winked. "Don't worry, babe. I'll be right back."

"You fucking better be," she said.

There was no more time for hesitation. Zach took off running. The girls stood by the open door, tense as animals at the slaughterhouse. They watched in anticipation as he closed in on the red SUV, knowing the creature could potentially swoop in at any moment.

A loud hissing noise came out of the compact fire extinguisher, making the girls jump.

"Sorry," Milk said. "Just making sure I can use this thing if I need to."

They all turned back to watch Zach slide under the car and begin frantically searching. It didn't take long for him to find the key and get inside the car.

"Yes!" LeeAnn cried, pumping her fist.

"He's doing it!" Nina said.

"Get ready," LeeAnn said, looking back at the girls.

As the car reversed toward the cabin, they all got ready. Once it was only a few yards away, they made a break for it.

"Shotgun!" Nina yelled, as they bum-rushed the SUV.

Nina pounced on the passenger seat while Milk piled into the backseat beside LeeAnn. Milk kept the fire extinguisher ready in case the horsefly was attracted by the movement of the car.

"Buckle up!" Zach said.

"Okay, let's go!" LeeAnn squealed.

Slamming his foot on the gas, Zach peeled out. The ladies clicked their seat belts in place as the car zipped down the driveway. The path was straight and long, so he quickly got the car up to fifty before he reached the end.

But just as the road came into sight, so did the beast.

The bloodstained creature's wings buzzed with fury. A bloody football-size rock hung in her hairy legs as she loomed over them. It seemed like the horsefly was aiming the crimson boulder directly at Zach.

"Oh shit!" Zach cried, jerking the wheel to the left.

The horsefly let the rock go and the car shifted simultaneously. The move was just enough to keep the boulder from hitting Zach. Instead, it crashed through the windshield and plunged into Nina's chest.

The momentum saw the stone burrow deep into her torso. A mixture of blood, vomit, and shattered glass flew throughout the car as they crashed into a thick tree trunk. The force of the collision stunned all passengers. As smoke billowed out of the engine, Zach tried desperately to turn the engine over.

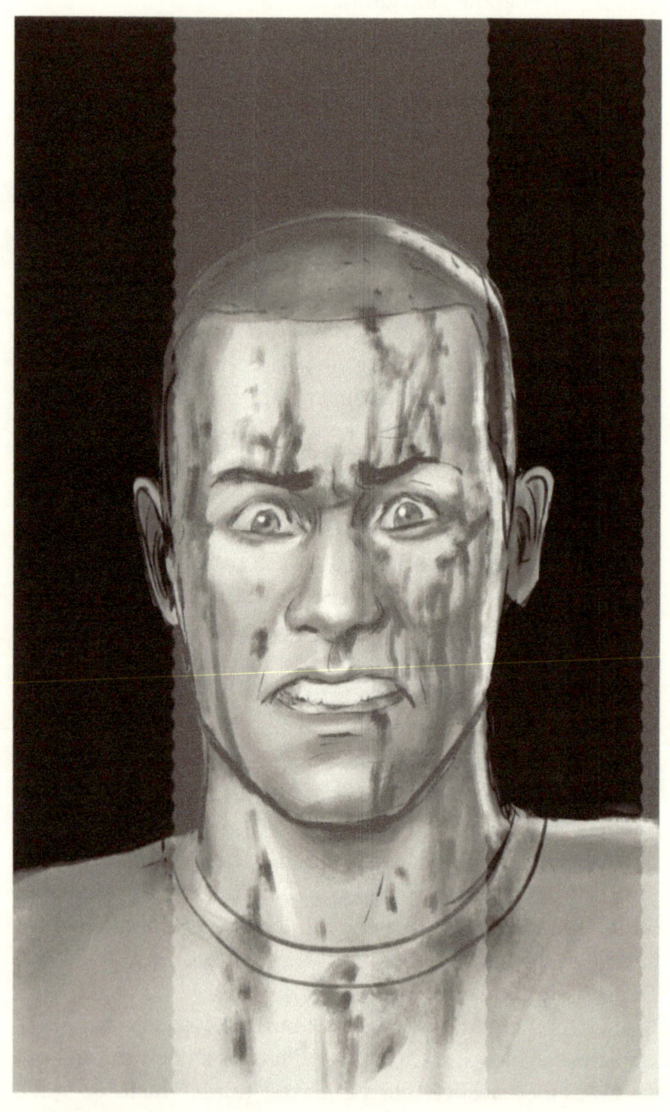

"Oh my God, Nina!" Zach screamed. "I-I'm sorry!"

A shiver of agony vibrated through her body as she violently choked. The puke and blood oozed from her mouth while her fingers clawed at the bloody half of the boulder that had punched through her torso. Nina's guttural moan urged Milk to take hold of the fire extinguisher.

"Zach, start the fucking car!" LeeAnn begged.

"It—it won't start!" Zach yelled.

"What are we gonna—"

Before LeeAnn could finish her question, the horsefly crashed through the passenger window with a piece of rotten wood. The window smashed, and the beast mounted the door. They all screamed as she stuck her mandibles through Nina's head, sending her blood spraying all over Zach's face and body.

Amid the deafening screams, they all naturally migrated out of the other side of the car.

"Run back to the cabin!" Milk said. "It's our only chance!"

The horsefly wasn't satisfied with just feeding on Nina. It made its way around the car, gore-dripping maw trembling as it buzzed toward them.

"Oh fuck, it's coming for us!" Zach yelled.

"Stay close!" Milk said.

She turned toward the beast as it approached them and activated the extinguisher. The thick, white powder poured out, creating a blanket of obscurity. The horsefly seemed confused by the synthetic mist, not willing to fly into it.

"Keep moving toward the door!" Milk yelled, continuing to unload the extinguisher behind them.

The horsefly buzzed around the growing cloud aggressively, but each time it tried to make its way around the fog, Milk extended it. When they finally reached the door, they slipped inside and slammed it shut. Zach promptly turned the lock.

"Get in the bedroom, keep quiet, and stay away from the door," Milk whispered.

As they approached the bedroom, Milk blasted the living room and outside of the hallway with extinguisher spray. They filed inside, and Zach closed the bedroom door and locked it.

"It smashed through the one upstairs," Zach whispered in terror. "It might come through this one too."

"That's only because it heard you or saw you through the glass," Milk whispered, hands trembling as she still held tight to the fire extinguisher. "Horseflies go off visual cues, warmth, the carbon monoxide we exhale, and occasionally vibrations." Milk looked down at the extinguisher again. "She seemed pretty confused by this. The chemicals must be throwing her off. If we just keep quiet in here, we should be okay. For a while anyway . . ."

They all sat in silence, sharing the same feeling of dread, listening closely as the sound of buzzing wings grew louder above their heads, and praying that they didn't come any closer.

DISEASE X

When Ruben awoke, the smell of blood and shit was overwhelming. The pain dotted over his forearms and face like a downpour of rain. As his vision came back into focus, he could see the pool of diarrhea surrounding his hips. The rotten scent tingled inside his nostrils as he examined the pus-filled bumps that covered his arms and hands. He groaned as the agony ran through his nervous system, deeper than the worst sunburn he'd ever felt.

But the speed and ferocity of his suffering was nothing compared to the circular sensation of the fury storming inside him. He'd done a lot of horrible things in his time, but he suddenly hungered to be worse—worse than he'd ever been before. He glared at the sharp axe that sat on the ground.

When he sat up, lumpy yellow vomit erupted from his mouth onto the pile of exploded horseflies dotting the shit-puddle that encircled him. Their tiny, vile bodies swirled in the gunk, ripped at the seams.

They fed to the death, he thought.

He summoned the will to get to his feet and staggered toward the weapon. As Ruben took hold of the wooden axe handle, he sensed the thirst for carnage rumbling in his heart.

There was nothing that would stop him from seeking retribution. From the second he'd awoken, he knew he was ready. He felt manic, like a windup doll that had been fully cranked.

They'll all fuckin' pay.

When he turned toward the door, he saw Whitney's motionless body on the other side of the barn. She was surrounded by her own puddle of blood and shit peppered with countless mangled horseflies. He recalled the beating he'd given her.

That felt so good. I want more . . .

He wasn't sure why his cock was hard. He wasn't thinking of anything sexual, but his loins burned uncontrollably. As he walked by Whitney's broken body, Ruben kicked one of the barn doors open. And the *only* thing he could think about was feeling good again.

DEATH CAMP

The gun's handle was still sticky from the peanut butter and jelly sandwich. But Toby held on to the piece like it was his only child. He glanced out the blinds of the cabin, looking for any sign of the creature.

"That-a boy," Jared said. "You're looking pretty comfortable with that thing now."

Toby's heart was still racing. The horsefly had forced them to divert off the trail. Instead of investigating the slaughtered horses on Wayne's ranch, they'd ended up at Camp Hawk—a place they were supposed to visit for a welfare check anyway. But after breaking into one of the vacant cabins, all Toby could think about was Wayne's violent demise.

Toby gripped the gun tighter. "Th-thanks, man. I appreciate you showing me how to fire it."

"No problem," Jared said. "I'm just glad you're willing to finally take a shot. It's the least you could do after dropping the walkie-talkies in the shitter."

"I said I was sorry."

"Well, you really fucked us. We could've had backup on the way by now." Jared approached the other window and checked outside. "But you know, I'm actually kinda glad we don't have them anymore."

Toby looked at him as if he were a recently committed mental patient.

"It's up to us now to take that son-of-bitch out," Jared said.

"What do you mean? We—we've gotta get the hell out of here, man. That thing . . . it fucking cut Wayne in half!"

"Exactly. We've gotta get payback for him."

Toby flailed his arms in agitation. "Dude, you fucking *hate* Wayne! You always whine about how he complains to us all the time about the people staying in that cabin. You said you think he's fucking his horses, for Christ's sake!"

"I might've hated him, sure. And it's very possible that he's taking liberties with those horses—that's probably why he was so damn emotional." He shuddered in disgust. "But it's the principle. It was our duty to protect that fucking crybaby, and all those wimps at the cabin too. I wanna save that girl with the melons. I bet she'd be mighty grateful if I slayed that fucking fly and saved her ass, don't you think?"

"This isn't a fucking game, man! There's plenty of pussy out there for you to impress. We need to—"

Jared stepped up to Toby. "It ain't about the pussy . . . It's about the *titties*."

"W-we can't go out there alone," Toby squealed. "I'll buy you a freakin' hooker when we get to the city! I—"

"Shut your goddamn mouth, sissy!" Jared yelled. "We took an oath, remember?"

Toby exhaled and went silent.

"To uphold the law and protect public safety in the area we serve. Now I'm gonna save those goddamn titties. You can either come with me or live with the weight of betraying these woods."

"Wait—what? You're *leaving*? Right now?!"

"We've been sitting in here all morning. We've gotta make a move at some point. Are you with me?"

A big glob of jelly hung off the side of the gun. Toby huffed, licked it off the barrel, and swallowed it. "Fuck it."

Jared grinned wide like he finally felt alive.

"Hell fucking yeah."

He opened the door carefully and scoped out the area of the campground.

"Get my back," Jared said. "Let's head toward the entrance. The main road is probably the best way to get back to the cabin. That thing can easily creep up on us in the woods."

Toby nodded. "All right."

"Let's move quickly."

Jared and Toby exited the cabin. The campground was fairly large, and as they made their way from the overflow of empty cabins, a short trail through the woods finally led them to the entrance.

Toby's heart was pounding as he gripped the gun.

"There's the main cabin," Jared said. "Holy . . . Looks like there's a car parked near the cabin!"

Please, God, don't let that fucking thing show up, Toby thought. *Please, just—*

The squishy sound under his foot made him pause. As he looked down, he grimaced in horror. The Pomeranian looked like it had been mummified. The emptied dog carcass already had plenty of flies and ants eating at it.

Toby winced, pulling his foot away from the mushy pile of rot. "Ahhhhhh!"

"Quiet!" Jared said, whipping around.

"That thing could still be around. We-we've gotta move!" Toby said. "This pup was just a fucking appetizer for that thing."

Glancing down at the rotten dog, Jared nodded. "Fair enough."

As they made their way around the cabin, the buzzing of many flies could be heard. The place looked more like a post-war battle bunker than an isolated lodge. Several windows were shattered, and blood stained the ground leading around the cabin.

"Oh, fuck," Toby cried.

His eyes sifted through the sickening carnage. The cuts on the body parts strewn about the area were tattered. They looked like they'd been sawed through.

A man's drained corpse lay on the ground, split down the middle, organs exposed below the horrified frown on his pale face. The flies hummed around, feasting on what remained of his innards. Through the broken window, Toby could clearly see more pieces of destroyed bodies. What looked like a woman's body lay defiled on a blood-soaked couch. She was missing her head and part of an arm.

"I guess we know why the Nettles never made it home," Jared said, finally able to get his jaw moving.

"My fucking God," Toby said. "What the hell happened here?"

THE NETTLES

DEATH CAMP CONTINUED

"Are you kidding me?" Jared asked, rolling his eyes at Toby. "You still high or just plain stupid? I mean, I'm no detective, but I do recall the giant fucking horsefly that sent Wayne to join his stable of sex-slaves in heaven. He's probably somewhere in the clouds, hiding from God, hunched over a horse with his cock in—"

"Look! Inside the car!" Toby said, pointing.

As Jared turned, he saw a child sitting inside the parked convertible. The preteen boy looked gone. He stared ahead blankly, giving no reaction to either of them.

Jared raised an eyebrow. "Holy shit."

They quickly approached the car, and Jared knocked on the window.

"Son?" Jared said.

Toby could see the keys hanging from the ignition. The car was already running. It was as if the boy were just waiting for one of his parents to rise from the dead, hop in the convertible, and drive away with him.

"We're here to help, kid," Jared continued. "Just open up the door."

After several attempts to get the boy to comply, Toby was starting to get antsy. "Maybe we should just break the window. We can't be waiting around for him to snap out of it. Who knows when or . . . if he ever will."

"You're right," Jared said. "We've gotta move. I'll bust out the back window."

He approached the passenger side and smashed the butt of his rifle into the glass. It shattered instantly, but before the shards could even hit the ground, the buzzing sound was upon them.

"Shit, watch out!" Toby cried. "It's back!"

Jared and Toby dropped back, looking for the source of the noise. They each scanned the surrounding area with their guns, but by the time they spotted the horsefly, it had already zipped by them and squeezed through the broken window. Blood splashed about inside as the vehicle rumbled violently, shaking side to side.

Several rounds erupted from Toby's handgun. The first bullet shattered the windshield and plunged into the boy's chest. The next two fired rapidly in succession but missed. As Toby unloaded the fourth in horror, he watched the bullet hit the boy directly in the mouth. With the child's jaw dangling from his face, a bloody mass of muscle twisted about in his mouth while the horsefly's sawtooth prodded him.

"You're killing the fucking kid!" Jared cried.

"I-I didn't mean to!" Toby said.

As the car continued to shake, the top suddenly started to drop back. The horsefly wrapped its spikey legs around the bleeding boy's quivering body and flew away before they could figure out what to do next.

"I . . . I shot him," Toby mumbled.

Jared was already hopping into the bloody convertible when he called out to his partner, "He's got bigger problems than a couple of bullet holes now." He whipped the vehicle around in reverse. When he finally located the switch for the drop top, it was broken clean off.

"Fuck," Jared mumbled.

Toby looked off into the distance as the horsefly disappeared with the boy's crimson carcass into the thick forest. "I fucking killed him . . ."

"Damnit! The roof switch is busted." Jared looked at Toby. "Hey! Snap the fuck out of it and get in!"

Shaking his head, Toby jumped into the backseat.

"Keep your goddamn eyes peeled." Jared put the car in drive. "If that thing comes back, you'll get your chance for redemption."

"W-what's happening?" Toby whispered. "We've gotta get out of here."

"You ain't wrong." As Jared wiped the child's blood off the steering wheel, he stomped on the gas and peeled out. "But first, we've gotta check on the rest of them."

ONSLAUGHT

The three of them sat in the bedroom, the atmosphere just as tense as it was defeated. Zach held LeeAnn tight, still devastated about what happened to Nina. Since they'd returned, he couldn't help but think about how he'd jerked the wheel when he'd seen the horsefly. In his mind, he'd chosen his life over hers.

"I . . . I didn't mean for her to . . ." He couldn't even manage to get the words out.

LeeAnn sniffled. "It was a split-second decision. There was no way for you to know that would happen."

He shook his head, lip trembling. "But it's still on me."

"What happened to Nina was horrible," Milk said. "But it was an accident. We've gotta figure out what to do next."

Zach stood up. The stress of everything was weighing on him. He couldn't stop himself from exploding. "There *is* no 'next'! You tell me! What the fuck are we supposed to do now?!"

Milk looked down at the fire extinguisher. "We do the only thing we can. Fight."

"But we don't stand a chance against that thing," LeeAnn said. "It's too powerful."

Working her way up from the bed, Milk approached the blinds and peeked outside.

"We're fucking done," Zach said.

"No!" Milk yelled. "Say whatever you want, but I didn't come this far to give up." She took a deep breath and let her hands rest on her belly, trying to calm herself. "I'm fighting for her. And if it's between my baby and that fucking horsefly, it's going to be my baby."

In the midst of the chaos, Zach had already forgotten that Milk was pregnant. Her determination helped reenergize him. Having a baby with LeeAnn was something he'd always wanted, and expected, to eventually happen. He'd planned on not only asking LeeAnn if she wanted to marry him but also if she wanted to start a family with him. Instead, Zach found himself in a much different position. The questions LeeAnn had posed rocked their relationship. But now, they'd battled and somehow found a way past it. Being reminded of those possibilities—that there was a bright potential future to return to—helped put things in perspective.

Zach nodded, trying to get his head back in the game. "Okay, you're right. I'm with you. But how? How are we going to fight that thing?"

"I'm not sure yet, but I know what we need isn't here," Milk said. "Maybe Wayne has some stuff on the farm that can help us. Whatever he has is better than what we have here."

"Well, running over there doesn't seem like the best idea either," Zach said. "Might as well paint targets on our backs."

"We still have some of this left." She returned to the bed and held up the fire extinguisher. "If it comes for us, I think I can fend it off."

LeeAnn looked at Zach for approval. When he paused in apprehension, she decided to speak up. "I don't want to go out there any more than you do, babe. But I think she's right. We're sitting ducks here. We've got a better chance on the farm. He must have weapons or—"

A thunderous thud could be heard in the distance.

"Shit, not again," Zach said.

Another loud thud.

"Shhhh," Milk said. "I think that's the front door."

The sound of wood splintering and a door flying open made Zach's guts squirm.

"Just stay quiet like we did before," Milk said.

The confusion hit when the sound of heavy footsteps drew closer.

"That's not the fucking horsefly," Zach whispered.

A pounding rang out from the other side of the bedroom door, each boom shaking Zach's chest to the core.

"You in there, faggot?" Ruben growled.

Milk held her finger to her lips.

"I know you're in there," he continued. "Open the god-damn door!"

Milk pointed to the window, and Zach and LeeAnn approached it, quietly sliding it open.

"Fine, I guess I'll open it myself!" Ruben roared.

The blade of the axe smashed through on the first swing.

"I'll chop you all to pieces!" he yelled.

When the axe connected a second time, it created an even wider hole. Milk sprayed the fire extinguisher toward the door, intentionally filling up the room. But the chemical cloud suddenly cut out.

"Damn!" she said.

Dropping the empty canister, she turned toward the window. When Milk got to the sill, Zach and LeeAnn were already outside. They quickly helped her out of the hazy room, closed the window and ran like hell.

***

The precum on the tip of Ruben's dick was different than normal. What might typically be a little splotch felt like a wet patch of gummy pus. As the thick smoke dissipated inside the empty bedroom, he saw a pair of Gen's panties beside her lingerie on the dresser.

I want that, he thought.

Memories of all the times they'd fucked flickered in his head. Her deep moans of pleasure resounded in his skull. Ruben still had no idea why he felt so violent and horny. It was as if his brain had been swapped out. Despite the anguish he felt, the rush of strange feelings excited him. He felt more dangerous than ever. Like man's rules didn't exist anymore. Like the world was his for the taking.

"Yeah . . . it's yours for the taking," he grumbled to himself.

When he staggered out of the bedroom and reentered the living room, he could see Gen's mutilated body laid out on the kitchen island. Her gory, open flesh called to him.

"It's all yours for the taking . . ."

IN AND OUT

When Jared pulled alongside the red SUV, he could see them through the broken window. The woman's face was mangled, and her blood was splattered everywhere. The violence obscured them some, and the massive rock that had caved in her chest had pushed them apart while also pointing them toward each other, but he still recognized the incredible hooters.

"Fuck," Jared said. "It got her."

"Man, this is freakin' crazy," Toby said. He kept his head on a swivel, just waiting for the horsefly to come buzzing out of nowhere and attack.

"That fucker's gonna pay." Jared clenched his teeth and shook his head.

"Dude, I'm serious, we need to be in and out of here."

"You think I wanna fucking be here?" Jared felt heartbroken as he pictured her bloody melons again. "Especially now?"

"I got a super bad feeling."

"Welcome to the club. We'll check the cabin, Wayne's place, and that's it."

As he pulled up to the cabin, Jared could see that the door was busted open. The puddle of blood that he'd spotted through the scope of his gun remained dried on the ground. Jared put the car in park and left it running.

"This looks promising," Toby said, raising his gun. He grabbed the rifle and handed it to his partner.

"In and out." Jared looked at him. "Same as when I stop by your mom's house."

Toby forced a smile. "Fuck you."

They both vaulted out of the car and up to the cabin's front door, guns drawn and ready.

"Forest rangers!" Jared yelled.

When they stepped through the busted front door, they could hear the grunting.

"Jesus fucking Christ," Toby mumbled.

As Jared looked at the pile of sawed-up woman on the kitchen island, he realized the headless, mutilated body was nude but for some bloody lingerie.

The man standing in front of the corpse was covered in pus-oozing sores. His red eyes glowed with lust and rage. With each thrust of his cock into the feminine porridge, the glistening lesions on his muscular body wept. The mixture of blood and infectional discharge glistened, riding the sweat down his body.

"That *definitely* wasn't on my bingo card," Jared said, the mere sight of the rancid love-making inducing a nauseous feeling.

"Hands up!" Toby yelled.

Jared was impressed that Toby was somehow less affected by the nasty display than he was.

Maybe I don't give him enough credit, he thought, putting his hand over his mouth, trying to hold down the vomit. *That child murder might have toughened him up.*

"I'm not fucking around! Step away from the carcass and put 'em up!"

The revolting man continued to pound away, the intensity in his eyes never wavering. He tore into the woman's destroyed body like a rabid cat playing with a mutilated mouse.

"W-what do I do?" Toby asked. "Shoot him, or let him finish?"

Jared grimaced.

"What?" Toby asked.

"Sir, we're not fucking around," Jared said, raising the rifle and focusing on the bloody man. "Stop, or I'm gonna have to shoot you."

The man fucked even faster now, digging his hands into her organs and squeezing them with all his might.

Jared let off a shot, intentionally aiming for the wall behind him. The idea was to spook him enough to pull him out of whatever trance-like state he looked to be in.

The man's moans of pleasure cranked up to a higher pitch as more animalistic grunting commenced.

"Shit . . . he really wants that nut," Jared said. "He didn't even flinch."

As the man released a guttural wail, they could tell that he'd finally blown his load. He slumped on top of the carcass and took in the moment of ecstasy.

"All right, now that you're finished, put your goddamn hands behind your back," Jared commanded.

The man lifted his face out of the dead woman's guts, his bloody grin leaking lumpy pus and crimson-tinted drool. He moved beside the island and stuck his hands out in front of him, surrendering.

"I said behind your back, retard," Jared said.

"C'mon, I'm not gonna hurt you," the man said.

Jared looked at the blood-caked cock, peppered with sores, and the coagulated cum hanging between his legs.

"Sick fuck," Jared said. "Looking like an old spotted ham and you didn't even have the decency to use a rubber?"

Toby shuddered.

"Slap the cuffs on him," Jared said. "I'll cover you."

"Me?"

"Yeah, I'm the better shot." He looked at the bloody man. "You hear that, hot stuff? I'm certified with this thing. Make one move and you'll be looking like your fuck buddy there. Understood?"

The man continued to grin menacingly.

As Toby closed in with the handcuffs, he grimaced at the sight of the man's gnarly body. His sores continued to ooze an off-white discharge.

"I wish I had some fucking gloves . . ."

When the cuffs got close, the man suddenly lunged for the woman's guts beside him. He retrieved an axe by the handle, buried inside the shimmering viscera. And just as he raised it to strike Toby down, the shot went off.

"Holy shit!" Toby cried.

The bullet hit the man in the throat, causing him to drop to the floor along with his weapon. The axe clanged against the ground before sliding away from the pile of his soiled clothing beside the injured man. Blood expelled from his gunshot wound as a sickening gurgle fluttered from his mouth.

"I fucking warned you!" Jared said.

"Ev-everyone's dying," Toby said, frowning.

Jared stepped around the island. "Quick, slap the cuffs on 'em!"

As Toby bent down, the man's bloody hand quickly slid into the pair of pants on the floor beside him. The switchblade appeared in the blink of an eye. Neither Jared nor Toby had time to react. The man ejected the blade as he whipped around and jammed it into the side of Toby's neck.

"Nooooooo!" Jared yelled.

He raised the rifle and fired a pair of shots into the grinning man's head, spraying his brains out the back, all over the tile floor.

But the damage was already done.

Toby slumped against the wall, grabbing at the knife still lodged in his neck.

Jared's eyes widened. "No, don't take it ou—"

Before he could finish his plea, Toby had yanked the blade out of his neck. Blood pissed out in a stream and ran down his uniform.

Jared grabbed a towel off the stove and slapped it against the gushing wound, trying to slow the bleeding. "Fucking shit, hang in there, buddy!"

A series of sickening gasps escaped Toby's throat as he turned a spectral white.

Tears streaked down Jared's face. "D-don't you fucking go. You hang in!"

Toby brandished his bloody teeth and reached into his shirt pocket. As he dropped the bloody joint and his lucky lighter into Jared's hand, both of them got even glossier vision.

Jared leaned in, listening to his partner closely.

"Don't let it . . . g-go to . . . to w-waste," Toby managed.

"You got it, partner," Jared said. "But you're gonna be able to smoke it yourself. We're gonna stop this bleeding and get you out of here. You hear me?"

Frowning, Toby locked eyes with him. "J-j-just promise you'll d-do one thing for me . . ." he begged.

Jared wiped his tears away and nodded. "Anything."

Spitting up more blood, Toby cleared his throat one last time. "P-promise me you'll kill that fucking horsefly."

THE REVELATION

"We need to eat something while we still can," Zach said, turning up the heat on the stove.

Milk watched him crack another egg and drop it into the pan while LeeAnn opened a can of corn beef hash.

"I don't know if I can," LeeAnn said. "I feel sick . . ."

"I'm not hungry right now either, but who knows when, or if, we'll get another chance to eat." He looked at Milk and then at her belly. "Especially you."

"That popping sound before . . ." Milk said. "It sounded like gunshots."

"We can only hope," Zach said. "Maybe Wayne finally made it back with some help."

LeeAnn's forehead crinkled. "But don't you think they would've come over here by now?"

"Yeah," he said. "I suppose so . . ."

"What if Ruben comes back?" Milk asked.

Zach looked down at the butcher's knife he'd laid out on the counter. "If he comes back, then I'll take care of him. But the thing we really need to figure out is how we're gonna get out of here."

"I don't think we can . . . Not until the horsefly's dead," Milk said.

"But it's so quick and . . . *vicious*," LeeAnn said. "How would we even be able to kill it?"

Milk set some plates on the table. "That's what we've got to figure out."

"You said you encountered horseflies on your farm," Zach said. "How'd you guys control them there?"

"Do they have some kind of weakness?" LeeAnn asked.

The memory from when they first arrived replayed in Milk's head. When she snatched the horsefly off Nina and tore its wings off. The fly crawled around on the ground, completely vulnerable.

"It would have to be the wings," Milk said. "That's her biggest advantage. If she came at us and we were able to injure her wings—or even slow them down—then we might just have a chance."

"But it flies around so fast," LeeAnn said.

"Right—because of her speed, we'd probably have to lure her in to even have a shot," Milk said.

"Then what?" Zach asked.

Milk shrugged. "I'm not sure."

Zach opened the fridge and looked through it. He made a face of disgust before closing it and looking through some cupboards.

"C'mon, this might be my last meal," Zach grumbled. "Is a little hot sauce too much to ask for? Wayne's such a weirdo."

"Why do you say that?" LeeAnn asked, stirring the hash around.

"Because . . ." Zach huffed. "All this guy has is freakin' maple syrup."

Milk's eyes lit up. "That's it! Syrup would work! Something sticky would probably gum up her wings! Then she wouldn't be able to move them fast enough to fly!"

LeeAnn and Zach grinned in unison.

"Maybe Wayne isn't such a weirdo after all," Zach said.

"You guys finish cooking," Milk said, approaching the stairs. "I'm gonna go down in the basement."

"Why?" LeeAnn asked.

"Before Wayne snapped on us, he told me that he'd stockpiled enough maple syrup down there to last him a lifetime," Milk said. "Hopefully, he wasn't just bragging."

"Okay," LeeAnn said. "But hurry back. This shouldn't take much longer."

As she descended the steps, loud groans escaped the boards. Various junk flanked the entire space. She searched for a light switch. When her fingers finally found it, a bulb shone light on the shelf to her right.

"Jackpot!" Milk yelled. "You guys, he wasn't lying!"

Several steel pails sat on the floor, and above them were countless jars of the amber gold. The sight of the sugary topping gave her hope.

"Guys?!" she called out again. Realizing that they probably couldn't hear her, she shifted her focus back to the syrup. "I guess now we've just gotta figure out how to use it, then."

"You ain't gonna figure shit out," an angry voice behind her snarled.

Terror immediately bubbled in Milk's guts. By the time she whipped around, the steel shovel pinged against the side of her head, stunning her and scrambling her brain.

"You're gonna die, bitch . . ." the voice continued.

As Milk's vision started to focus, the details of Whitney's gnarly face did too. The knots and lumps of battered tissue were discolored. Her flesh was severely beaten into a deep shade of purple that would've made Milk wince if she wasn't already. Her mouth was full of broken teeth, and the shape of her head was monstrous—tissue enflamed in several different directions, while broken facial bones caused other areas to dip. There were crusty caps of pus on the countless bites that littered not only her face but her entire body. The hardened gunk was repulsive.

The only thing more distracting than Whitney's vile body was the agony ringing in Milk's head. She watched Whitney raise the shovel with a flaming rage in her eyes. When the steel smashed flush against Milk's face, the violent blow quickly abbreviated her scream.

"Milk, the food's ready!" Zach called out.

She could hear his voice faintly, but it sounded like he was getting closer.

"Hey, are you all right down there?" Zach asked.

Milk spat out blood, along with several pieces of her teeth. She grabbed at her belly and whispered a plea to Whitney. "My baby, please . . . I have a baby."

Whitney grinned, brandishing her own busted enamel. "Not yet, you don't."

She aligned the point of the shovel with Milk's little belly bump and readied her foot like she was preparing to dig a grave. As a sadistic gleam twinkled in her eyes, Milk realized that she was.

"Please, don't," Milk cried.

The motion was the same as if Whitney were trying to cut through earth. When her foot jammed down on the top of the tool, the sharp tip penetrated Milk's gut. The squishy sound of the shovel blade further slicing into her innards with each successive stomp intensified.

Milk let out an otherworldly wail, one that penetrated the old wooden walls of the house and beyond. After all, she was screaming for two.

"What the hell's going on down there?" Zach called out.

The shockwaves running through Milk's body numbed her as Whitney used the shovel to widen the hole in her gut and scoop out some of her organs. When she pulled another shovelful of gore, Milk could see the upper half of a mangled fetus quivering on the mini pool of slop.

Her baby—or what was left of it—was the last thing Milk saw before she nodded out.

STICKY SITUATION

"I've gotta go down there," Zach said, taking a deep breath and swiping the butcher knife off the counter.

As Milk's horrified wails suddenly died, Zach watched LeeAnn grab another knife from the block, but she looked unsure if she'd even have the guts to use it.

"But what if it's the horsefly?" LeeAnn asked in terror.

"Then I guess we're fucked either way," he said. "Stay here. Just keep quiet until I'm back."

As Zach rushed down the stairs, his heart rattled with adrenaline. He didn't think it was the horsefly—he hadn't heard the creature's familiar buzz. He felt fairly certain that he would've recognized it. But a profound fear of the unknown now resonated inside him. He was afraid to find out the source, but for LeeAnn's sake—and Milk's—he knew he had to.

Holding the knife steady, Zach crept down the old steps and was immediately confronted with a stomach-turning scene. Milk's twitching body lay near the bottom of the stair-case. The light shone on the massive hole in her stomach and her crimson organs strewn about.

Whitney stood at the bottom of the staircase holding a bloody shovel, looking like a deranged zombie. She raised the shovel with one hand and used the other to toy with herself.

"Come down here and save your little friend," Whitney said, grinning with her busted teeth. "Don't worry, I'm not jealous. It's like I told you on the phone—I'd still love to suck your cock. I'd gobble up the entire fucking thing."

The sudden sound of a shot being fired echoed throughout the basement. A small piece of Whitney's leg blew off the bone, and she dropped to the ground, shrieking in pain and grabbing at her wounded leg.

"Do not fucking move!" a male voice said.

A man in a forest ranger uniform approached her but turned his gun on Zach.

"Drop the fucking knife!" the ranger demanded.

Zach dropped the blade and held up his hands.

"Officer, please, w-we need help," Zach said. "She—she went psycho and killed my friend, and there's a giant fucking horsefly after us!"

He nodded. "It's Ranger."

"My name's Zach. My girlfriend, LeeAnn, is upstairs. We mean you no harm. We're just trying to . . . to get the fuck out of this place."

Whitney made a quick move for the shovel again, and the ranger shifted his aim to her good leg. When the shot hit her this time, it blew the back of her calf away. She let out another wail of horror.

"That's what you get for fucking around," Jared said.

The ranger put her hands behind her back. Zach spotted several lengths of rope hung up near the staircase. He quickly grabbed one and helped the ranger secure Whitney's arms behind her back.

After they both caught their breath, Zach wiped the sweat off his face. "So who are you?"

"I'm Ranger Myers," he said, wiping the blood off his hands onto Whitney's shirt. "But you can call me Jared."

"Thanks for stopping her, Jared," Zach said.

The ranger pointed at her scabs. "I can tell you're not one of the crazy ones because you don't have these nasty-ass spots all over you."

Zach nodded. "I'm glad." He looked at Milk, who lay motionless on the ground. His eyes welled with tears. "Can I please check on her?"

"Have at it."

Zach squatted to try and comfort Milk, but she was already gone. He wanted to cry. Neither Milk nor her baby deserved the brutality that Whitney had unleashed on them. He forced himself to think about LeeAnn.

She needs you to be strong, Zach thought. *I've gotta hold it together. For her.*

"Looks like she's gone," Jared said.

"She was a fucking cunt that deserved to die!" Whitney screamed. "You all fucking deserve to rot. I'll kill every fucking one of y—"

Jared used the butt of his rifle to smash her in the face. Her nose cracked and the back of her head smacked against the hard wood, silencing her. He dragged her limp body to the side of the staircase, where the other lengths of rope hung from a hook. Winding the rope around Whitney's bloody legs, Jared ensured that the deeply disturbed woman wouldn't be going anywhere.

"Crazy bitch," Jared said, glaring at her. "Christ, she's vile. She's just as whacked as the other one."

When Zach looked around, he suddenly wondered how so many people had made their way into Wayne's basement. His heart started to race as he thought about the murderous horsefly.

"How'd you get down here?" Zach asked.

Jared turned and pointed to the open bulkhead door. "I was gonna check the house, but I heard screaming coming from down here."

Zach rushed toward the open door, his anxiety spiking. He thought about the horsefly's hairy legs, murderous tendencies, and razor mandibles before quickly closing the bulkhead and locking it.

"Don't want any more unexpected visitors," Zach said, turning back to Jared.

"That's for damn sure." The ranger licked his lips and sniffed the air. "Is . . ." He sniffed a couple more times. "Is that food I smell?"

"Yeah."

"Would you mind if I joined you?" Jared asked. "I haven't eaten in, like, a day."

Zach looked over at Milk's dead body, still holding back his emotions. "I don't see why not. It's not like she can anymore."

MESSAGE FROM GOD

Bzzz-rrrruuuumm-zzt, the horsefly thought.

As she sat perched on a tree near the lake, the horsefly looked at the collection of bodies and parts piled up on the edge of the waterfront. She knew her work was almost done. She turned her attention to the night sky, when a question suddenly came to her. It was like she was meant to ask it.

Bzzz-hhhhumm-bbbbzzzt? she asked.

A lone shooting star soared through the sky. God had given her the answer she needed. The rage that continued to fester inside her blood-filled body would never end. The species that posed a threat had to be annihilated.

She glared at a section of one body in particular. The head, shoulders, and single arm of a man that she'd cut into sections and transported to the lakeside. The man's face was peppered with countless bites from her sisters—those who had given their lives to transfer the enlightenment into his species.

The horsefly buzzed in disgust, annoyed with his failure. With such enlightenment, she imagined the man would've made an impact of some sort—that he would've continued on with God's work. But he'd failed, only proving that his species was worthless and pathetic. There was no doubt that they all deserved to be eradicated.

Zzzzzuuurrrrt-bbbrrrrr-zuuum!

A faint splashing in the water distracted the horsefly from her internal rant. She looked at the many white sacs nestled in the tree branches. They made her feel closer to reaching her goal.

She looked at the failure of a man again. Her heightened senses picked up the faint smell of food cooking in the distance. Some of his comrades were still alive. With each additional murder, she grew stronger. The blood of many had given her not only an excess nourishment but also an excess confidence.

Bmmm-zzzuumm-bbbbzzzt!

The humans had started out with the numbers. But slowly, one by one, they'd each fallen. They would all fall in time, and that time had almost arrived.

She moved over to the pile of body parts and sifted through it until she found the one that still had a meal to give. As she sawed into the dead flesh, the blood didn't ooze as quickly as she would've liked, but it still oozed. The horsefly lapped up the warmth. She would be at full strength when she descended upon them.

The final battle was near.

LAST SUPPER?

"Did she say something about sucking your cock down there?" LeeAnn whispered, annoyance tainting her tone.

Zach smirked. "Yeah."

LeeAnn shook her head. "That bitch."

"What, are you jealous?"

She pouted, triggering him to hug her.

Zach wouldn't admit it, but it felt comforting to see his woman care. In this case, LeeAnn's jealously was actually a good thing. It reaffirmed that she cared again. It helped him realize that, as fucked up as their trip had been, some positives had come out of the dominant darkness.

"You've got nothing to worry about," Zach said. "If you saw Whitney, you'd know what I mean."

Flashes of Whitney's tongue sliding over her broken and bloody teeth made Zach shudder.

"She's the one who has something to worry about."

Zach looked at Jared, who stood near the window, then back to LeeAnn. "You mind doing these dishes while I talk to him?"

"Yeah, I guess we need to figure out what the hell we're gonna do." LeeAnn gathered the dirty dishes from the table, placed them in the sink, and turned on the water.

***

As Jared stood beside Zach in the kitchen, he cautiously looked through the window at the open barn door. There was a trail of blood near the entrance.

"That might be exactly what we need," Zach said.

"What do you mean?" Jared asked. He looked back at LeeAnn washing the dishes. "You don't have to do those."

"It's rude to just eat his food and leave dirty dishes," LeeAnn said.

Jared nodded. "That would be true . . . but he ain't coming home."

Zach raised an eyebrow.

"Wayne's, uh . . . he's tending to the big farm in the sky now," Jared continued.

"Oh . . ." LeeAnn said, slowing down the washing before deciding to keep on with it. "I'm gonna just finish them. It's somehow calming for me."

"Anyway . . ." Zach said, turning back to Jared. "I say it because before Milk died, we'd started putting a plan in place to fight that thing."

"I'm sorry . . . Milk?" Jared asked. "Like dairy?"

"Yeah," Zach said. "The girl downstairs, that was her name."

"Oh." Jared nodded. "No, that's cool. Just a little different is all."

Zach looked back out at the barn. "Anyway, I think I might have an idea."

Jared held his hand up. "Well, before you say it, I'm obligated to tell you something."

LeeAnn stopped washing.

"I have a working vehicle outside," Jared said. "You can leave right now if you want to."

"What? That's fucking amazing!" LeeAnn squealed. "We should go, right now, all of us! Night would be easier to make a—"

"I can't go," Jared said.

"What?" Zach said. "Why not?"

Don't be a fucking sissy, Jared thought.

It took everything for Jared not to cry in front of them. He acted like a hard-ass, brushing off the horrible things he'd seen. But when the dead bodies flashed in his head, he shuddered. Wayne's torso ripped in half, the mangled little boy and his massacred family, the bloody melons, the manic, bite-riddled man, the destroyed carcass on the kitchen island, the knife in Toby's neck, the gaping wound in Milk's belly, and the leg meat that he'd blown off Whitney's legs. After everything, Toby's final words were still with him, echoing in his head over and over.

P-promise me you'll k-k-kill that fucking horsefly, he'd said.

"I took an oath," Jared said. "To protect these lands and those within them. And I failed. But you didn't take that oath. You're both free to go. But I made a promise to my partner." His voice cracked before he steadied it. "I'm gonna get that fucking maggot. That son-of-a-bitch is *mine.*"

There was an awkward silence that filled the room.

"Babe . . ." LeeAnn said.

"Do you mind if I speak with my lady for a moment?" Zach asked.

"By all means," Jared said.

Zach took LeeAnn off to the side, but Jared could still hear their whispers.

"If you want to leave, we'll leave," Zach said. "But I think I have a plan that'll work. You know I'd never put you in danger if I wasn't sure."

"I don't know . . ." LeeAnn said, biting her nail.

Jared watched as she made eye contact with him—it was like she could feel the pain transferring from his eyes to her soul.

"We—we can't just leave him behind, can we?" Zach asked, glancing back at Jared. "He kinda saved my ass downstairs."

LeeAnn shook her head. "It's his choice to stay. We can't make him leave with us."

"No . . ." Zach said. "But we can help him fight. We can see this thing through. We can stop that horsefly from killing any more people. Plus, it might be our safest bet."

"How so?" LeeAnn asked.

"You remember what that thing did the last time we tried to drive out of here. Nina—"

"Folks, I appreciate the sentiment," Jared said. "But do what's best for yourselves. I take no offense."

Zach and LeeAnn looked at each other.

LeeAnn sighed and shook her head. "This better be the best fucking plan ever."

INTO THE NIGHT

Bbbbbzzzzzzzzzzzzz:

The horsefly ascended above the tree line. In the distance, she could see the faint glow coming from the lit lanterns inside the barn. Sensing her remaining prey was near, she approached the structure, while the anger inside her reached its pinnacle.

The woman lying on the ground outside the entrance of the barn was savagely wounded. Amid the woman's injuries were the speckling of dots over her disfigured face and body—the scars of the horsefly's chosen; those who had sacrificed their lives to transfer knowledge, to lead the woman down the path of God. And she'd pissed it away.

Buuuuzzzz-rrrrfffftt-mmmuuzz! the horsefly thought.

Proving just as useless as the man, this woman deserved the same sentence: eradication. The bound and gagged lady didn't deserve the sweet blood that was oozing from her wounds. The horsefly would see to it that her blood went to a good cause—that it would be used as nourishment to boost her farther down the path of enlightenment that God had guided her to. As she sped through the air faster, she could see the horror on the woman's face, but the horsefly didn't feel sorry. That pathetic species deserved *only* anguish.

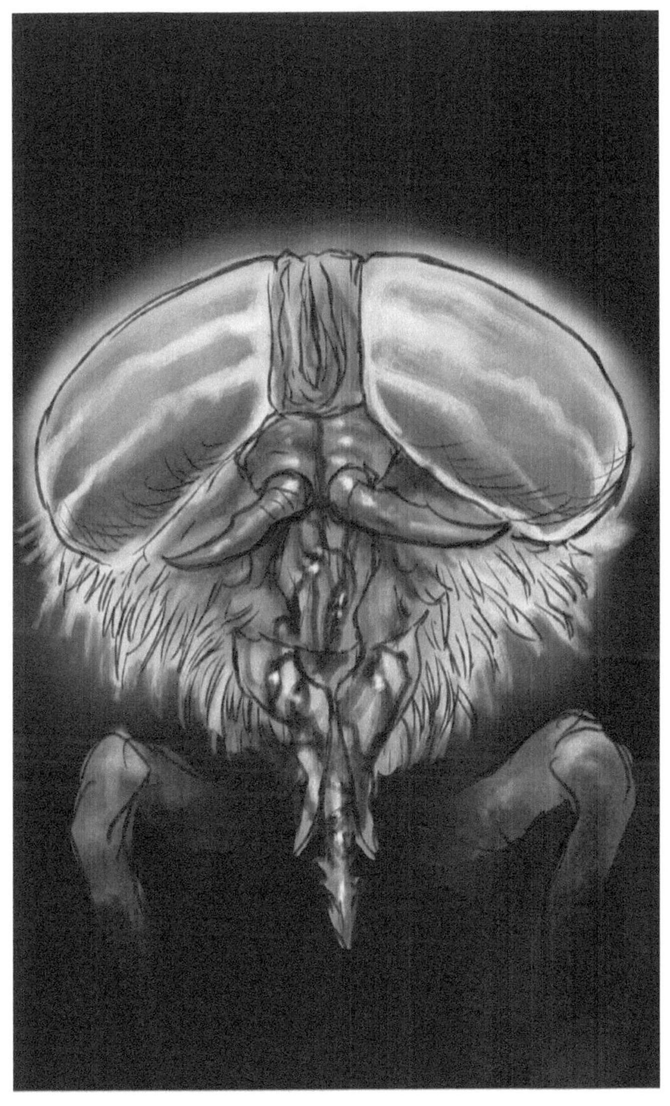

Zipping into the woman's personal space, the horsefly suddenly heard yelling.

"Pull her in, now!" a man's voice shouted.

She didn't understand the cries and stayed focused on the lady. But as the horsefly drew closer, the rope around the woman's body was tugged, dragging her into the barn, prompting the horsefly to pounce on her even quicker. As she pinned the woman down in the entrance of the structure, her mandibles sawed through the rope and into her torso. Blood flowed generously, and as tears dripped from her prey's eyes, the horsefly started to lap up the warmth.

A TIME FOR VIOLENCE

LeeAnn's heart was racing as she waited for Zach to make the call. They stood on the upper level of the barn, hidden behind stored hay bales. She glanced down at Jared as he took cover behind the tractor, gun aimed at the entrance, rope by his side, waiting for the signal.

The big uncapped bucket of maple syrup in her hands was heavy. Zach had dumped even more of the mason jars filled with the sticky sugar into his bucket but could still handle the weight with ease. She looked directly below, carefully watching the massive horsefly plunge its sawtooth into Whitney's belly.

"Now!" Zach yelled.

They both dumped their buckets of maple syrup directly onto each of the horsefly's wings. The gooey, amber substance coated the wings and the top of the giant insect's body. The creature seemed stunned as Jared opened fire with the rifle.

The first shot plunged deep into the horsefly's body, while the next one skimmed its eyeball, blowing a piece of it clean off. The enraged bug went berserk, trying to flap its wings toward Jared as he unloaded several more rounds.

"Fuck, it's—it's not dying!" Zach said. "Quick, open up the door!"

LeeAnn rushed to the wall on the upper level of the barn and removed the wooden latch from the hay-loading door. She looked through the opening at the massive pile of hay they'd arranged on the ground below.

"Be ready," Zach said, lifting a pitchfork.

As he launched it down toward the fly, the beast was finally able to dismount Whitney. The steel tines missed the horsefly, instead burrowing into the side of Whitney's abdomen, causing her to cry out.

Despite moving forward, it seemed that the horsefly had realized its wings were no longer operable. It was now using its legs to quickly dodge the bullets that Jared was firing, closing the distance between the two of them.

"Jared!" Zach yelled. "She's closing in on you, head for the ladder!"

"Shit!" Jared yelled as the nasty bug's prickly legs scuttled closer.

The ranger dropped his gun and made his way around the tractor with his eyes on the ladder. LeeAnn prayed that Jared was faster than he looked. If things went to shit, like they seemed to be, the plan was for Jared to climb the ladder, and they would use the soft hay below as their emergency escape plan.

But Jared didn't even reach the second step when the horsefly's razor mandibles cut through both the ladder and Jared's thighs. He wailed in pure agony as he fell into a heap, landing on a stockpile of gas canisters stacked near Wayne's tractor. Several of the containers had spilled over, creating a small puddle around him.

The potent smell of the gas crept up through the hole in the upper level of the barn that both LeeAnn and Zach were watching through. Jared flipped himself over, feeling the gasoline burn his leg stumps, and faced the beast. The quivering mandibles inched closer.

"You're one ugly son-of-a-bitch," Jared mumbled.

As the horsefly mounted him, he looked at the stockpile of gas and the growing mixture of accelerant and blood that encircled him. Chuckling to himself, Jared reached into his top pocket. He slipped Toby's fat joint between his lips and readied his lucky lighter.

"Get ready to jump—"

The injured ranger's words came with pain attached as the horsefly's unforgiving mouth bones slashed deep into his nether regions. As the horsefly began to defecate liquid shit it carved through Jared's cock and balls. His eyes widened, and he prepared himself.

LeeAnn and Zach both approached the door and stared down at the massive pile of hay. They watched helplessly in angst as Jared raised the lighter, smiling as he glared at the foul insect like a fierce warrior ready to die in battle.

"Puff . . . puff . . ." Jared flicked the lighter. "Blast!"

The explosion boomed right when LeeAnn and Zach simultaneously launched themselves out of the window. Pieces of the wooden boards flew in all directions as they descended into the pile of hay. The shower of wooden splinters had found their flesh, but as they got their bearings and checked each other, they were relieved that the gashes were all superficial.

They both looked back at the burning barn as the long flames inside continued to grow. LeeAnn was half relieved and half saddened.

"Fuck . . ." she whispered. "Jared . . ."

Zach shook his head, looking at the flames. "There's no way he'd make it out of there . . . him or that horsefly. At least he got what he wanted."

LeeAnn shook her head. "Yeah, I guess."

The sun was beginning to come up in the distance, and to LeeAnn, it felt not only like the dawn of a new day but of a new life. A life where she would be grateful for every peaceful moment and take nothing for granted. She pulled the car keys that Jared had left with her from her pocket.

"Should we wait . . . or get out of here?" LeeAnn asked.

"I think it's time to go," Zach said with a tiny smile.

They staggered around the side of the flaming barn. As they headed toward the front of the property, a thought suddenly hit Zach.

"Oh, wait! First, I've gotta—"

But before he could finish his thought, a voice called out from the side of the smoky structure.

"You ain't going anywhere!" Whitney yelled.

She slowly staggered out of the smoke. In addition to her countless wounds, Whitney's face was now also horrifically burned. Pitchfork in hand, she somehow managed to stumble toward them. With the spikes aimed at Zach, she wailed like a savage invading a village.

"You think you're too fucking good for me?!" Whitney shrieked.

LeeAnn pushed Zach out of harm's way and avoided Whitney's thrust. When she got her footing, she palmed the car keys between her fingers. She thought back to the countless power punches she'd watched Zach throw when he hit the heavy bag, seeking to harness the same strength. As Whitney regained her balance, LeeAnn threw her hand forward so fast it looked like a rocket. The point of the key hit Whitney in the eye with such force that it tore into the backside of the orb.

As LeeAnn pulled the bloody key out, Whitney dropped the pitchfork, falling to the ground and clasping at her face. Blood shot out around her hand as her other eye bugged out of her head. LeeAnn quickly pushed her backward and mounted her, raising her bloody spiked fist again.

"He's spoken for!" LeeAnn yelled, unleashing a rain of vicious blows.

The bloody key stabbed into Whitney's face over and over, creating a new puncture wound with each strike. As the messy key cut through her flesh, Whitney continued to cry out. But when LeeAnn drove the jagged steel into her neck several times, her cries bled away and the warm red started to flood.

As Whitney's involuntary body spasms slowed, so did LeeAnn. When the tremors of death concluded, LeeAnn got up from the ground and cleaned the blood off the key. Her hands were still shaking from the fresh surge of adrenaline when she looked at Zach.

"Baby, are you okay?" Zach asked.

"L-let's get the fuck out of here," LeeAnn said. "For real this time."

"No," Zach said.

She furrowed her brow, confused and still terrified.

"Just one more thing," Zach begged.

"Babe, seriously?!" LeeAnn stomped her foot. "You're really pressing our luck."

"She was the last one," Zach said. "Jared already told us that Ruben and Wayne are dead."

"I know . . . but I just can't be around this fucking place any longer." She sobbed. "It feels cursed!"

Zach moved in and brushed his fingers over the side of her face and her hair. "Please, just one more thing. It would mean a lot to me. I'll drive. You can relax."

She sighed. "I won't be able to relax until we're out of here."

"You've gotta trust me on this."

LeeAnn shook her head, handing him the keys. She was still frightened, but one thing was for sure: she could count on Zach to protect her. He'd risked his life to keep her safe. He'd earned that much. She answered him with her eyes and a passionate kiss.

HEADING OUT

When Zach pulled the bloodstained car up to the cabin, the sun had risen. His heart was pumping, even though he knew it shouldn't be.

"Go around back, to the fire pit," Zach said. "Wait for me in the hammock."

"Where are you going?" she asked.

"I'll be right out. Two seconds, I promise."

"All right."

As LeeAnn made her way around the house, Zach entered the bloody cabin again. He ignored the stains and remnants of violence that saturated what was supposed to be a tranquil space reserved for relaxation.

What a crock of shit that was, he thought.

He rushed up the stairs and into the room they'd been staying in. Locating his backpack, he sifted around before retrieving the ring box. He rushed back down the stairs and out through the back of the cabin.

LeeAnn was waiting in the hammock, just as he'd asked her to. When he slowly approached her, he saw that she still wasn't picking up on what was happening. But as he dropped down on one knee, her eyes glossed over. She put her hand over her mouth.

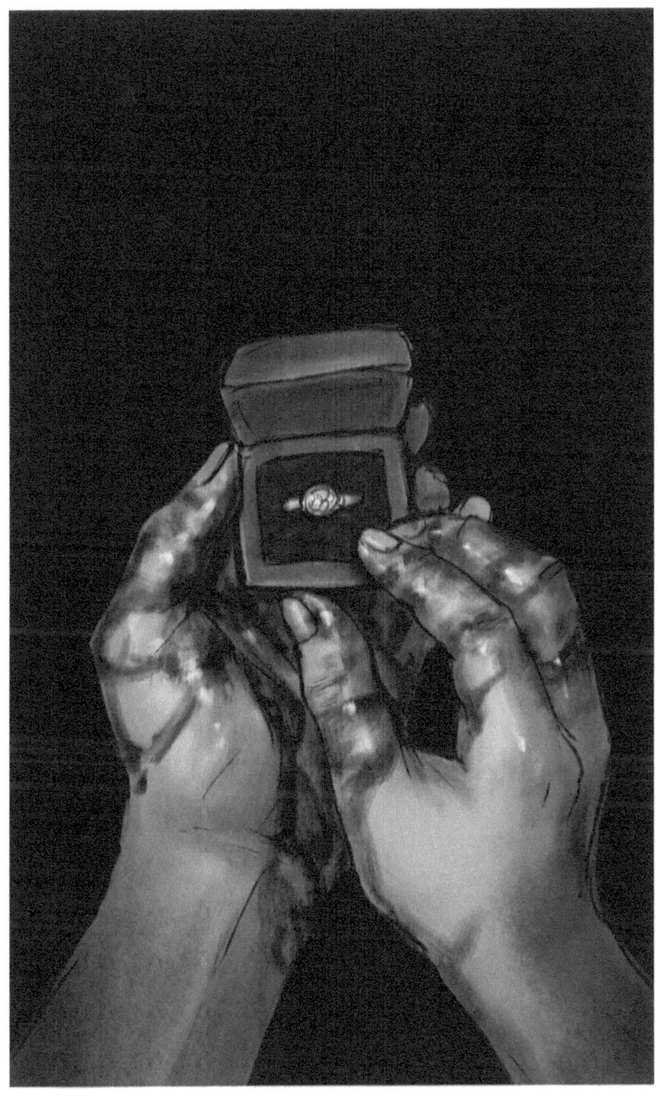

"Oh my God," LeeAnn whispered.

Zach opened the box, and the stone glimmered in the sunlight. His lip started to quiver.

"Before any of this started, I believed in us," Zach whispered. "I knew no matter what happened here this weekend, that you and I were meant to grow old together." A tear ran down his face. "I knew if I could make it through this trip and still be by your side, then buying this ring was the best decision of my life. Now . . . I didn't quite see it going down like this . . . but, baby, if you and I can make it through this fucking weekend together, then we can make it through anything. What do you say?"

LeeAnn broke down, tears running down her face as she lifted the ring out of the box with shaking hands. After she slid it onto her finger, she pulled Zach into the hammock.

"You're the only one I need," she whispered.

As he held LeeAnn tight, she cried into his chest. Zach lowered his head. When his lips touched hers, the horror and vile memories in the back of his head were a little easier to deal with. Because now he knew that the lips against his—the only lips in the world he'd ever wanted—were the last ones he'd ever feel.

SOMETIME LATER

THE AFTERMATH

What kind of ninny sets up an experimental research lab containing a dangerous specimen one room away from the shitter and then leaves the goddamn window open? William Fence thought, waiting impatiently in his office. The image of Carl Simmons' slumped-over corpse hanging in the doorway flashed back into his mind. *Fucking numbskull got exactly what he deserved.*

The sweat under William's man boobs was as moist as it'd ever been. He looked down at his shirt in disgust, using a tissue to try and absorb some of the sweat.

"I told you to have them turn on the damn air-conditioning an hour before I arrive," he said.

"I . . . I did, sir," his assistant, standing against the wall, replied. "I told them twice, an—"

"Well, tell them again!"

"Of course."

The second William's assistant exited, he immediately scratched at his legs like a depressed dog. Lifting his pants, he looked inside. The skin was still enflamed and itchy as hell. He'd been dealing with it ever since the horsefly had shit on him and Carl.

"Goddamn rash," William grumbled. "The thing looks hideous! Sure is taking its time clearing up. I'm—"

He stopped himself. It had finally hit him—the idea he'd been waiting for.

"That's it!" he yelled, a smirk slithering across his face. "A rash! It's perfect! It's—"

His "a-ha" moment was interrupted by the turn of the handle. When the door opened, another man holding several video tapes entered.

"It's about time, Gerry," William said. "Where the hell have you been? I haven't got all day to wait around. Why the hell can't anyone just be punctual anymore? It's the bare fucking minimum."

"Sorry for the wait, Mr. Fence," Gerry said. "But there's still a lot of questions about what happened out by Mount Archer. There's a lot of cleanup that had to be done, and a lot that still needs to be done."

"Tell me something I don't know." William scoffed. "That's what I'm paying *you* to handle—and paying you quite handsomely, I might add."

"I know," Gerry said, approaching the VCR sitting atop the television. "I'm doing my best to handle everything properly."

"Well, do better." William looked at the handful of tapes in his clutches. "What are those?"

"They're part of the documentation of the aftermath that I picked up. Dr. Cruise's assistant sent them through to us for review."

"Dr. Cruise." William shook his head and scoffed. "The moron that left the bathroom window open. I'd like to wring her neck."

"I'm afraid that's no longer possible."

William frowned. "What do you mean?"

"I mean she's dead," Gerry said.

"Oh." William's confusion transformed into ire. "Were there any other casualties?"

Gerry turned on the TV and pushed the tape into the VCR. "Several . . ."

"Seriously?"

"Yeah."

William smacked the table in frustration. "Did they re-cover the horsefly's carcass? At least give me that much."

"No . . . but the evidence on-scene leads us to believe it was probably burned."

"'Probably' doesn't work for me, Gerry! I need concrete answers."

"We're still working on determining that."

"And what about survivors?"

"Just a man and a woman."

His glasses were beginning to fog up. William removed them and cleaned the lenses with his shirt. He took a deep breath, doing his best not to get himself too worked up. "I assume you've delt with them already."

"Not exactly. Unfortunately, the girl's uncle is a police of-ficer. They went directly to him and reported the situation. I'm not sure now's the right time for any *action* to be taken."

When Gerry pressed play, several people appeared on the TV. There were two women on a couch sixty-nining, while a man jerked off, ejaculating onto a second man's eye mask and mouth area.

"Whoops," Gerry said. "Wrong tape."

"One from your private collection, eh?" William sniped.

"Noooo, it's another tape that was taken into evidence from the people at the cabin."

"Suuuuuuure."

Gerry quickly read the label on the side of the next tape. "Ah, this is it. Sorry."

He played the new tape. The TV showed a cameraman following Dr. Cruise as she approached a lake bank. Several pieces of mutilated bodies were strewn about on the ground. She and another one of her associates had a ladder propped up against a tree that arched over the water.

She climbed the ladder toward a doughy sac attached to a branch, then balanced while carefully holding a needle in one hand. She approached the large, white egg, stuck the needle into it, and depressed the plunger.

"Remember Carl," her associate said off-camera. "Make sure you put the proper dose."

"Stop comparing me to Carl!" Dr. Cruise snarled. "I would never be so reckless."

"Fucking Carl," William quipped, recalling his blunder inside the lab. "This is all because of that asshole."

"I just want to be safe," the associate said.

"I am safe, damnit," Dr. Cruise said. "Trust me, I was tasked with doing his autopsy, and what a fucking mess that was. The *last* thing I want is these eggs hatching."

"You and me both," the assistant said. "Is it true that you pinched a loaf in the lab and left the window in the shitter open, and *that's* how the horsefly escaped?"

"Don't be silly . . ."

"Well, how did it get out the—"

"Oh fuck," Dr. Cruise interjected.

"What? What is it?!"

"Those other branches." Dr. Cruise pointed past the eggs in front of her toward several others in the distance that she clearly had not initially noticed. "There's more than these . . ."

"Fuck," her assistant said. "Should I load up a few more needles really quick?"

"There's no need . . ."

"Why?"

"Because they've already hatched."

As the words came out of her mouth, the sound of the buzzing became deafening. A small army of mammoth, hairy-legged horseflies zipped across the lake. Their massive, glowing eyes filled with rage, their saw teeth ready to find flesh.

When the camera fell, so did part of Dr. Cruise's head. The bloody gash ran from cheek to cheek, sawing her cranium off at her jawline. Her tongue jiggled as blood spewed out and her eyes rolled up into her head.

The screams of the humans and the buzzing of fly wings grew louder. The sound of meat being poked and prodded echoed through the TV speakers.

"And it just kinda keeps going on like that for a while," Gerry said.

William swallowed, afraid to ask the question. His heart pumped furiously with anticipation. "Where are they now?"

"They gathered up all the bodies and had them—"

William pounded the table again. "Not the people, you fucking dunce! The horseflies!"

Gerry huffed, seemingly not looking forward to answering the question. He bided his time before finding the courage. "Unfortunately, we have no fucking idea."

THE LOST TAPE

THE

RASH

COMING IN 2026?

ABOUT THE AUTHOR

Aron Beauregard is an older guy who checks very few
boxes. However, the one box he *does* check is the pool
box. He has to maintain a house and the goddamn swimming pool that came along with it. It took him thousands
of dollars and many years to master. And while these days
he opens the pool fairly smoothly, there are still many bat-
tles he must wage—mainly with the primary villain in this
book. The massive horseflies that come out of the woods
and flock to the pool each season to spoil his nude seren-
ity/neighbors' nightmares were the inspiration for this
book. And very much like *Horsefly*, the fight isn't over.
It'll *never* be over.

ONLY AT ABHORROR.COM

AB HORROR FUN FACT

After going super viral in July of 2023, Aron Beauregard's "Playground" books have sold countless copies and ruffled serious feathers. The incendiary series has triggered the masses in such a way that the author still receives the occasional death threat. If you'd like to know what all the fuss and outrage is about, check out "Playground" and "Playground: Child of Divorce." If you'd like to submit a death threat, those are also very much appreciated as the author has been living based on spite alone for some time.

HORROR WITHOUT BOUNDARIES

AB HORROR CHALLENGE

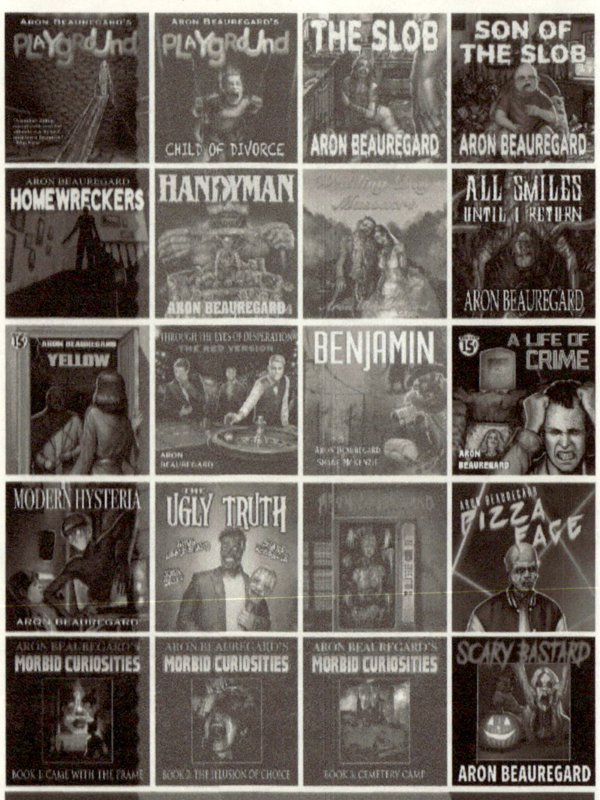

To participate in the AB Horror Challenge, simply read or listen to any Aron Beauregard book, then take to social media and share your reaction. Talk about how you felt surviving the nastiest or the most emotional parts in your videos or posts, and then tag the author for a chance at free signed books and more! To increase your chances, TikTok videos are highly encouraged! Tag the author: @ABHorror

FOR SIGNED BOOKS, MERCH, AND
EXCLUSIVE ITEMS VISIT:

ABHORROR.COM

FILM & TV RIGHTS

Horsefly was written with the big screen specifically in mind. For inquiries on obtaining film or television rights, please email:

AronBeauregardHorror@gmail.com

SERIOUS INQUIRIES ONLY.